Not the End of the World

Rebecca Stowe

Not the End of the World

Rebecca Stowe

Pantheon Books   New York

"Two Years Later" from
The Poems of W. B. Yeats: A New Edition
edited by Richard J. Finneran
(New York: Macmillan, 1983)

Library of Congress Cataloging-in-Publication Data

Stowe, Rebecca.
Not the end of the world / Rebecca Stowe.
I. Title.
PS3569.T6753N67   1992   813'.54—dc20   91-53084
ISBN 0-679-40945-9

Manufactured in the United States of America
First American Edition

Book Design by Fearn Cutler & Silvia Ribeiro

Has no one said those daring
Kind eyes should be more learn'd?
Or warned you how despairing
The moths are when they are burned?
I could have warned you; but you are young,
So we speak a different tongue.

O you will take whatever's offered
And dream that all the world's a friend,
Suffer as your mother suffered,
Be as broken in the end.
But I am old and you are young.
And I speak a barbarous tongue.

W. B. Yeats, "Two Years Later"

Not the End of the World

Rebecca Stowe

Chapter 1

"A man," I said when Miss Nolan asked me what I wanted to be when I grew up.

The Bridge Ladies tittered like a bunch of fat little birds.

"She's crazy," Grandmother said and clicked her tongue and wanted to know if any of the Bridge Ladies had ever seen such a sullen little thing. "She says she wants to be the first woman governor of Michigan," she cackled as she began pulling at her cards with her red-tipped fingers. "Can you imagine? Whoever heard of such a thing?"

The Bridge Ladies tittered some more and Miss Nolan peered at me over her cards, the tip of her white rubber nose peeking over the pansies, and pointed out that I couldn't be the first woman governor of Michigan if I were a man.

"You didn't ask what I was *going* to be. You asked what I *wanted* to be."

Mother gasped and Grandmother glared but Miss Nolan just laughed. "I think perhaps you're too honest to be a politician, Maggie," she said, lowering her cards and revealing her white rubber nose in all its grotesqueness. "You'll have to learn some diplomacy."

I blushed and hung my head, angry with myself for not being able to look at her, to look at the repulsive white thing stuck on her face like a plastic Mr. Potato-Head part. Grandmother always used Miss Nolan as an Example. "That's what will happen to you," she'd threaten, chasing me around the house with a tube of sunscreen, shaking it at me and saying, "All right, Miss Smarty-Pants, just don't come crying to me when you have to have your nose removed."

Mrs. Tucker snorted. "Pee-pee envy," she said knowingly and the Bridge Ladies shrieked like crows.

"May I go now, please?" I asked, thinking I'd die if I had to stand there one more second, being polite while Grandmother insulted me and Mrs. Tucker made snide remarks.

"And where are *you* off to, Miss Ants-in-the-Pants?"

That was Mother. When Grandmother was around, I couldn't tell them apart, they were always insulting me and calling me stupid names, names so stupid even my friends didn't use them. Miss Ants-in-the-Pants! What was I, three?

"The beach," I said and Mrs. Tucker said I should call Cindy; she didn't think Cindy was doing anything after her guitar lesson. Or perhaps she was. Maybe she had ballet. Or maybe she was going water skiing in Rick Keller's boat. She just couldn't keep up with her. Why didn't I have any Outside Activities? Outside Activities build character. Cindy had plenty of *that!*

I shrugged and said I thought I'd like to be alone. They all laughed and Grandmother fanned herself with her cards and made heaving noises.

"She thinks she's Greta Garbo," she said. "Whoever heard of such a thing? A twelve-year-old who *vants to be a-lone?*"

They laughed some more and Mother informed them I had a paper to do for summer school.

"Summer school!" Miss Nolan said. "Why, Maggie, I had no idea you were so dedicated a scholar."

"I'm not," I said. "I'm being punished."

"Oh," Miss Nolan said, blushing a bright red ring around her rubber nose, "I'm so sorry!"

Not half as sorry as I was, I thought, wishing Mother would dismiss me so I could run to the beach and hide. I felt like a prisoner, having to stand around while my executioners had a quick game of cards before taking me out back to stand me against the picnic table and shoot me.

They lit cigarettes and arranged their cards, as if I weren't there, as if I hadn't asked to be dismissed, as if I were just an invisible vapor they only paid attention to when they needed something to laugh at. Grandmother was glaring across the table, angrily watching Mother lay out her dummy hand, as if it were Mother's fault she didn't have the cards Grandmother wanted. She'd yell at her later, when the Bridge Ladies had left and before Daddy came home; she'd scream at her for not having bid correctly, for having given her the wrong clues.

"May I go now?" I asked again and Mother nodded glumly as the Bridge Ladies smiled fake smiles and smoked and slapped their cards on the table. "C'mon, Goob," I shouted and she bounced out from under the couch and we flew out the door. "I hate them," I told Goober, "I hate them." I loathed them, despised them, wished they'd all step on rusty nails and get lockjaw. It would serve them right.

Here it was, almost the end of the world, and all they did was sit around smoking cigarettes and drinking martinis and playing bridge with a deck of pansied cards when at any minute the whole world could be blown up into a zillion pieces. People were building bombshelters and storing cans of fruit and choosing the people they'd take with them into their safe little caves, the people who would survive the atomic blast and create a new world, and all these stupid women could think about was building character through ballet. Character, schmaracter. What difference did it make if you were dead? What difference did it make, anyway? You built up character all the time you were a kid and as soon as you were an adult, you tossed it out the back door with the coffee grounds.

Well, pretty soon they'd be singing a different tune. Pretty soon, they'd all be fried and not just their noses, but everything, right down to their toenails. They'd be sizzled like hot dogs on a grill, sputtering and popping and bursting their seams.

"I wish we could move to Oregon," I told Goober as we crawled under the shrubs overlooking the breakwall, to check to see if any Enemies were on the sand, sunbathing. Oregon was the only state that might not get zapped, but my parents wouldn't move. They thought I was crazy.

"Margaret, where do you come up with these ideas?" Mother would moan when I'd show up at the dinner table with a list of essentials for surviving the atomic blast. "School," I'd say and she'd wonder why, if that were the case, no one else's children were making such a fuss about it. I'd shrug and look to Donald for support, but he was too busy thinking about getting dinner over so he could hide in his room with his stupid girlie magazines to care about the end of the world. I hated those magazines, with the bare naked ladies grinning at the camera and their boobies hanging out in public; it was disgusting and I wish I'd never found them in between Donald's mattresses.

Donald and I used to be best friends until he became a teenager. We still stuck together when we had to do "family" things, but outside the house he pretended like he didn't know me. "Right, Donald?" I'd say and kick him under the table, but he'd just grunt. Ruthie would start squawking and crying, certain that when the Bomb hit, Mother and Daddy would take Donald and me away, leaving her to fry alone. "You're going to *leave* me!" she'd sob. "The Russians are going to get me!" I'd grab her pudgy little arm and tell her to knock it off. "The Russians don't care about *you*," I'd say and then she'd really start sobbing. "Nobody loves me!" she'd wail. "Nobody wants me!" She'd flap her arms and drift off into her little birdworld, squawking and screeching and pecking at her plate with her nose. "Now look what you've done," Mother would say, shoving a plate at me. "You've set her off again." "*Me?*" I'd scream. "Why is it always *me? I'm* not the one putting missiles in Cuba!" Then Daddy would try to demand peace—he'd thump his fist on the table and stare at me and tell me that was enough. He'd call me "Young Lady" and that would set *me* off. "Don't *call* me that!" I'd shriek and run from the table, through the kitchen and up the stairs. I'd lock myself in the bathroom, waiting for the All-Clear, waiting for someone to come and tell me everything was OK, I could come out now, it's not the end of the world.

But it never happened.

Chapter 2

ONLY MRS. Prittle, the neighborhood spy, was at the beach, sitting in her red and white striped beach chair like a leather vulture, waiting to pounce on anyone who ventured down the steps to the sand and to chase off anyone who didn't belong at Edison Beach.

I didn't want her to see me; if she did I'd have to go over and be polite, and being polite was what I hated third in the world. Mrs. Prittle asked too many questions—she was always poking and prying and even though she was just trying to be nice, to make conversation, it drove me crazy because I always ended up telling her things I didn't want to tell her, just because she was so pushy. She meant well, I guess, but she made me all squirmy.

She didn't have any kids of her own, just a snappy, hairy dog with some Chinese name, Ping-Pong or something. After the Red Chinese started threatening to take over the world, she told everybody the dog was *really* Japanese, like she was afraid people would think it was a spy.

The only way to avoid her was to crawl through the shrubs to the Kellers' hedge and then slide down the sand onto their beach and then sneak across the Wilsons' beach to the Sisks'. The Sisks' beach was my private hideaway, cut off by two high and long cement breakwalls, extending all the way into the water so nobody could walk on their beach. The Sisks never used their beach and if they came out at all, it was to sit in their pretty white gazebo, set up on a little lump of a hill, separated from the beach by a row of stumpy evergreens. They could sit up there and watch the freighters chugging past without getting sand in their shoes.

The Sisks were pretty nice people, and I don't think they would have minded too much if they'd caught me hiding on their beach, although Daddy would have had a fit. "That's Private Property!" he'd say. "That beach belongs to the Sisks! You have your *own* beach, you've got no business trespassing on somebody else's!" Daddy was a fiend for Private Property. He didn't get mad much, but that was one thing that could really get him going. Forget the Lord's Prayer; he wasn't forgiving *anyone* who trespassed against *him*. He even had a NO TRESPASSING sign on his den—as if anybody would want to go in it, anyway; it was just a dark little room with a big old table where he said he "worked," but what he really did was play with the tin soldiers he had locked up in the cabinet behind his armchair. God only knows what he would have done to me if he ever found out I'd sneaked in there—probably boiled me in oil or tied me to a stake outside the house with TRESPASSER written across my forehead in my own blood, and all because he didn't want anyone knowing he played with soldiers. Big deal. Tom Ditwell's dad had a set of *dolls*, and although he said he had them just in case he ever had a daughter, nobody believed that baloney. "Is he some kind of sissy?" Donald asked Mother and she blushed and

9

said certainly not, Harry Ditwell was *all man*. I asked her how *she* knew and she blushed again and said she ought to know, after all, they were in Dance Club together.

The Sisks' house was the nicest along the Lake—a long, rectangular stone house painted a very light blue, like the Lake in the early morning when the sun was just rising over Canada. I wondered if they'd done it on purpose, if they'd sat out in their gazebo every morning with their painter, waiting for just the right color. They had white cast-iron pillars with blue and white morning glories circling around them, leading up to a balcony that extended the length of the house. In one corner, they had a huge telescope, pointed towards Canada. Sometimes, I'd sneak down to their beach at night and hide behind the evergreens and watch Mr. Sisk as he stood on the balcony, looking at the stars. I could see Mrs. Sisk sitting inside, playing solitaire as she listened to classical music on their hi-fi, and it seemed so tender, somehow. So quiet and peaceful and tender and I wished I was their daughter. I would imagine myself standing on the balcony, looking through the telescope while Mr. Sisk taught me how to pick out Orion the Hunter and how to find the rings around Saturn. My parents didn't know anything, or if they did, they weren't sharing. Whenever I'd ask a question like, "How do airplanes stay up in the air when they're so heavy?" they'd laugh and say, "You're in the *sixth grade* and you don't know *that?*" and I'd feel so humiliated I'd skulk off to the beach with Goober and I'd never find out the answer. Mr. Sisk wouldn't laugh at my questions, I just knew it.

Ever since the trouble at school, I'd spent more and more time hiding out at the Sisks'. I felt safe there, not only on their beach, but in their wonderful backyard. It was like a fairyland: two whole blocks long, and filled with graveled paths and statues spurting water from fish and cupids, just like some English lord's garden. They had all sorts of little buildings back there: a log cabin and a gingerbread play-house and a shrine with a statue of the Virgin Mary in it. I thought it was a shame they didn't have children to enjoy their park and sometimes Goober and I would go back there and look in the windows of the little houses, but the only one I ever went in was the shrine.

There was a dusty velvet-cushioned seat in there, where I'd sit and confess my sins to the statue, even though I didn't know if it would do any good, because I was only an Epis-copalian. "*High* Episcopalian," Mother always said, which made me feel sorry for all the people who went to St. Matthew's and were Low.

I didn't go to church at all any more, not since the trouble. I was too bad. Grandmother said I was possessed by the Devil and unless we got him out by my thirteenth birthday my soul would be lost for ever, at least what was left of it. Once the Devil got in, she said, he never let go; he burrowed into your heart like a tapeworm and made it all black and rotten. That didn't sound right to me, but Grandmother said that was because the Devil had already got inside and gob-bled up all my good parts, and even if I went to church it wouldn't do any good because it was Too Late.

I didn't think God liked me very much. He was always punishing me. I must be very evil inside, I thought, deep down where only God and Grandmother and Mother could see it, because I was always getting punished, even when I wasn't doing anything bad. It was as if I was getting punished for something I'd done ten years ago, or something I'd prob-ably do in the future and I made God so mad He'd reach down from the clouds, pull me up by my scruffy hair, shake me around like a party favor and then toss me in a heap on the sunroom floor. And it didn't work both ways—I got punished when I was bad and even sometimes when I wasn't bad, when I was just trying to be a human being. But when I was good, there was no reward. Sometimes good things happened to me. Before the trouble, I got chosen to be the school reporter for the *Herald Ledger;* I got to go to their offices twice a month and meet the reporters and type up my stories on a big, noisy typewriter. But when good things happened, they had nothing to do with me. It wasn't a reward for being good, it was more like a gift, an act of grace, given not because I deserved it but because God was in a good mood that day.

Maybe that was why my parents never insisted on my going to church with them on Sundays. Donald was an Acolyte and Ruthie sang in the junior choir and Mother was an Altar Lady. Daddy only went when it was his turn to be an usher—he liked to collect the money. Sometimes, when I watched them getting all dressed up, I felt kind of left out, but I was too terrified to go. I was sure I'd walk in and Reverend Phillips would point his finger at me and start screaming "The Devil is amongst us!" and everybody would turn and stare and then they'd all attack me and beat me to death with their prayerbooks.

It frightened me, all that talk about the Devil, which was why I would sneak over to the Sisks' shrine all the time, to try to get an answer out of their statue. "Why would he want me?" I'd ask her, but she just stared benignly, as if it didn't matter and what was I so worked up about? "Well, how would *you* like it?" I'd ask, which was a stupid question; she was a saint, what did she know about devils? It really made me mad—if the Devil had my soul, wasn't he supposed to make some sort of pact with me, to offer me something for the use of it? Wasn't he supposed to give me something to satisfy my earthly greed so he could take my dirty little soul when I died? I didn't think he could just pick and choose, just go around grabbing infant souls without their having a say in it. I didn't like the idea of being possessed, but I might have considered making a pact with the Devil if he'd offered to turn me into a boy.

I hated being a girl. It was what I hated first in the world. "Better get used to it," Mother always said, giggling as if it was funny, but it wasn't. When I was little, when I'd say my prayers at night, at the end I'd say, "God bless Mother, Daddy, Donald and Ruthie and everybody else in the whole, wide world including Goober and please let me be a boy when I wake up." Now, I just said, "And please don't let there be a war," because it was too late, I'd already started my periods and sprouted breasts, real ones, not little lumps like everyone else, and I even had to wear a real bra, with wire in it, not a Gro-Cup. It was what I got, I suppose, for wanting to be what I wasn't.

Ginger Moore thought I should have a sex-change operation. "Maybe you could get Christine Jorgensen's old thing," she said and we wondered what happened to it: did he/she keep it in a bottle of formaldehyde, like those pig fetuses at the carnival? Did she keep it in a velvet box on her mantelpiece? Did she have it frozen in case she changed her mind and wanted it back? Or did she just toss it out like a bad memory?

"I don't want a *thing*," I told Ginger, "I just don't want to be a woman."

She didn't get it. If I didn't want to be a woman, then I had to be a man, and in order to be a man I would need a thing. If I didn't want a thing, then what *did* I want?

"I don't know," I said and she said I was crazy.

Chapter 3

THEY all thought I was crazy. Sometimes I worried that I was, but that was a good sign because real crazy people don't think they're crazy, they just think they're Napoleon.

"It's a wonder you have any friends," Mother used to say when I still had some. "You must become a different person when you leave this house. Jekyll and Maggie."

Actually, I was six different people, but I wasn't going to tell *her* that. They already thought I was crazy and they were just looking for an excuse to get rid of me. If I'd told them I had six different parts, plus a part that wasn't really mine, they'd have packed me off to Lapeer faster than you could say "Nuthouse."

It wasn't craziness—*The Six Faces of Maggie* or anything like that—I didn't black out and then wake up dancing naked on a pool table in the back room at Lyon's or anything. I was perfectly aware of all the parts and I knew when they were going to take over: there just wasn't anything I could do about it. I kind of winced and said, "Uh-oh," and waited for the you-know-what to hit the fan.

I kept them in an imaginary chest of drawers. The outside was a beautiful lacquered chest with two big doors painted with gold and blue flowers. Behind the doors there were six drawers, where my personalities lived when they weren't with me.

Maggie was me, the real me, the me only my best friend ever got to know. I didn't have a drawer, because I was always present, so I guess the chest was me.

Katrina was the part of me who thought she was adopted. She was a little girl, and when I was little, she'd run around the neighborhood telling all the neighbors that she was left on the Pittsfields' doorstep and her real mother was a Dutch prostitute. "Wouldn't you like a little girl like me?" I'd ask all our childless neighbors and Mother would have a fit. "A Dutch prostitute!" she'd moan, running upstairs to the strongbox to get my birth certificate in case anybody wanted to check. "Where do you come *up* with these things?"

I didn't know. I constantly accused my parents of wishing I'd never been born. "You didn't want me!" I'd shriek as I ran through the house with Mother chasing behind holding a wooden spoon full of fudge for me to lick, saying, "We did! We did! We tried *very hard* to get you!" "Ya," Katrina would shout from the top of the stairs, "and zen vhen you got me you vanted to send me back for a refund!"

Trixie was the name I gave to the mischievous me, the me that was playful and full of life and silliness. Trixie was the one who sang, "I'm Gonna Wash That Man Right Outta My Hair" in the McKinley Talent Show and who went to parties dressed in a hula skirt and who would do anything on a dare. She was the one who used to be popular, and one who could mimic anyone and who made Daddy laugh so hard he'd cry when she'd parade around the living room doing Grandmother imitations. Trixie didn't come out much any more, not since the trouble at school. It was hard being popular when everyone hated you.

The bad one was Margaret, as in "Margaret Sweet Pittsfield." She was the bully, the mean one, the one who'd smack her friends over the head with a Coke bottle if she didn't get her own way; the one who plotted and gossiped and said horrible things in the slam books. She was dirty minded and she was the one who always wanted to play sex games with her friends. She even had fits, but they were emotional instead of epileptic. She was the one who made me seem crazy. When Margaret took over, no one could get in, not even me—I'd watch in horror as she went wild, attacking anything or anybody who came near her. "Don't you *touch* me!" she'd snarl and that was how I knew she was coming. "Don't you *touch* me!" she'd spit, backing up and hissing like a snake. "Don't you dare touch me!"

Then there was Sarah. What a whiner she was. Boo hoo hoo. She was also the sweet part, the part Mother liked best, but I hated her. She was weak and mealy mouthed and a Good-Do-Bee, like some kind of twelve-year-old Melanie Hamilton. Weakness was to be avoided at all costs, so when I was feeling Sarah-ish, I'd run to the beach faster than a speedboat skimming across the Lake. I'd fly down to the Sisks' breakwall and climb over and let her have her stupid cry.

She was the good girl, the kind and loving one. She didn't get much exposure in the real world, but I liked to make up stories about her, little tales of loneliness and longing, with sad endings because no one would come and save her and she didn't have the strength to save herself. She'd always be left, floating down the Lake on a chunk of ice, or trapped in the woods with the Pervert, and nobody knew what happened to her because nobody really cared.

I only had one male part and that was Cotton Mather. Not the real Cotton Mather, just a guy I named that because he was such a Puritan and so righteous. Cotton Mather was in charge of Morality. Since I had none, he was always telling me to tie myself to a chair and throw myself into the Lake to see if I was a witch. "Let your conscience be your guide," the song says and that's great if your conscience is Jiminy Cricket, but it's not so great if it's some wrathful Puritan who wants to carve a B, for Brat, on your chest.

Cotton Mather said that everything that happened was my fault and that if I had been good, bad things wouldn't have happened to me. "You deserve it," he always said. Once, when Cindy was having a luau on the beach and we were all sitting around the bonfire, happily singing "Michael Row the Boat Ashore" while Cindy tried to play her stupid guitar, he said, "Do the world a favor and throw yourself in." He was really a pain in the you-know-what.

In the top drawer, there was Peggy. Peggy wasn't really a part of me, she was just this little girl who hid in my secret chest. She never came out, she just stared at me from the drawer and all I'd ever seen of her was her eyes. I didn't know who she belonged to. She was somebody else's kid, who got tossed away and ended up in my drawer. Sometimes, when I was upstairs hiding under the eaves, I'd imagine the chest and open the doors and there she'd be, just those eyes, staring out at me. She was terrified, but I didn't bother her. I just let her hide in there and I figured some day she'd come out and tell me who she was.

Margaret hated her. Margaret hated everybody, but she especially hated Peggy. Every time her eyes started peeking out, Margaret came rumbling out like a tank. "What a dink!" she'd say in disgust. "What's *her* problem?"

I think she was tortured. I think she was tortured as a little girl and had to fly away and ended up in my chest. "What a bunch of baloney," Margaret said. "It takes *years* of torture to turn somebody into nothing but a pair of flitty eyes." But no it didn't. It only took once. It only took once for adults— when Mrs. Greenwell got attacked by a man in the parking lot at Eastland and ended up having to go to a rest home, nobody said, "What's *her* problem? She only got raped *once!*" "It's different for kids," Margaret insisted, "they don't remember." But yes they did. Peggy did. And I felt sorry for her, having to live in somebody else's life.

It was kind of a strain, having all those different parts, all clamoring to be dominant. Of course none of them got along and as soon as one gained control, the rest would start screeching and yelling and making an uproar, all except Sarah, who just wrung her hands and cried. There was never a moment for me, Maggie, to rest, to get away from them, except when I was at the beach or in the Sisks' shrine. No matter what I did, I made one of them unhappy and I always had to hear about it.

I told Miss Dickerson, the social worker I had to see after the trouble, about Margaret and Cotton Mather, but not about the others. She thought it was all very interesting— her eyes got all bright, as if she were thinking, I've got a live one here! But I assured her that I wasn't one of those split-personality people. It wasn't as if I'd show up for breakfast and say, "Hi! I'm Cotton Mather. Got any gruel?"

When I told her that, she nodded and said, "Um hmmm," and made a couple of notes in her book. "And when did you first meet Cotton Mather?" she asked, trying to sound indifferent, but I knew she couldn't wait to get out of the room and put it all on her tape recorder.

"I didn't *meet* him," I told her. "He's always been there. I just started *calling* him "Cotton Mather" when I read about the

Puritan and he seemed a lot like that part of me that was always nagging and saying, "Bad, bad, bad, if you weren't so bad nothing bad would happen to you.'"

"Did something bad happen to you?" she had wanted to know but I wasn't falling for that.

"Getting into trouble is bad," I offered and she thought about it for a while. I hated it when she was silent, when she sat there like a stone, trying to make me squirm, giving me the Silent Treatment, trying to make me beg for attention. I wouldn't do it; I'd die before I'd break the silence, I'd let the voices inside tear me to pieces before I'd give in.

"Do you think that what happened with Mr. Howard was something that just *happened* to you?" she finally asked and I wished I *were* a witch, so I could zap her into a slimy snail and toss her out the window into the flower bed, where Mr. Peabody could smush her with his hoe when he weeded the garden.

I knew what she was after. She wanted me to admit that it was all my fault, that I had *made* it happen. That I made it all up and that there was never any danger, that I was evil, just an evil girl trying to ruin a nice man's career, that I was like those horrible, lying girls in *The Children's Hour*, who accuse the teachers of being queer. She wanted me to tell her that he didn't *do* anything to me so she could exonerate him and warn all the other teachers about me. She'd go to some teacher meeting and stand up on a platform and say, "Watch out for that wacko Maggie Pittsfield. She's evil and she's out to destroy teachers!" They were always on the lookout for that sort of thing, and I decided Miss Dickerson was just pretending to be kind so she could trick me into confiding in her. When I trusted her she'd run out of the room screaming, "Liar! Pervert! Lock her up!"

But she didn't say anything. She just sat there, watching

me with that calm, soft, wet-eyed face of hers, and I decided I hated her. I hated her and her so-called sympathy. It was her job to get me to talk and if being gentle didn't work, they'd send for some fat Russian woman who would shine lights in my face and poke me with electric sticks and fill me full of truth serum. "Confess!" she'd shout, smacking me over the head with her electric pointer. "You made it all up!"

"What happened with Mr. Howard?" Miss Dickerson asked, still gently, and I wanted to scream. I didn't know what to do. I didn't want to lie any more; the lie itself was unimportant and since they hadn't seen fit to chop Mr. Howard into a million pieces and feed him to the seagulls, the lie was beside the point. But I couldn't tell the truth—the truth was much worse than the lie. To say that he pushed me was nothing. Teachers pushed and smacked and slapped kids every day. Tom Ditwell had lumps like sand dunes on his knuckles from getting smacked so much with a ruler. Of course, he got most of his lumps at Catholic school, and maybe that was why his parents took him out and put him into public school, where it was supposed to be against the law to beat up pupils. But the law didn't stop anyone from whacking some bad kid, and usually nobody said anything, figuring they'd deserved it anyway and why go home and complain about getting punished only to get smacked again when your parents found out what you'd done?

Miss Dickerson just kept sitting there patiently, making me crazy. If I were her, I'd be shaking me and shouting, "Answer me, you little brat!" It made me uncomfortable, sitting there in silence, it made me want to start running around the room and pulling all the first-aid supplies from the cabinet, to hurl bandages against the walls and smash aspirin bottles on the floor. It was probably part of the game—if she could make me nervous enough with her silence, I'd have to break it by saying something and whatever I said, no matter how innocent, could be used as evidence against me.

I worried what they'd do if Miss Dickerson said I was crazy. Could they lock me up in the loony bin, with all those long-haired shrieking women in straitjackets? I'd seen *The Snake Pit*, I knew what insane asylums were like. I kept thinking about the scene where Olivia de Havilland is trying to get away from someone and she ends up locked in with the real berserkos, and they're all grabbing at her and shouting and tearing at her like witches, as if they wanted to pull her apart and eat her up. It was horrifying, worse than Reform School, where the worst thing that could happen was the tough girls from Detroit would beat you up and turn you into a Greaser.

Chapter 4

ALL that was during the regular school year, when I had to see Miss Dickerson three times a week. Now that I was in summer school, I only had to see her once a week and it was actually a relief to get out of Mr. Blake's class for an hour every Friday, even if it meant having my insides probed by a head-shrinker.

I hated summer school. It was boring. All we had to do was write one paper, the paper I was supposed to be working on. The *Detroit News* did an article on heroes: they asked a bunch of famous people to write about their heroes and Mr. Blake thought that would be a good idea for us, too, especially since most of us were in summer school for being bad or stupid and maybe if we had a hero, someone to look up to, we would be better. I thought it was dumb; as if Irma Gibbons, who was the only person I had ever met in my whole life who really *was* stupid, wrote a paper on Einstein she'd turn into a genius. Baloney.

I didn't have a hero. The famous people in the article

chose presidents and baseball players and generals, for the most part, although one writer guy chose Spinoza and Confucius. I thought it would be fun to choose someone Mr. Blake had never heard of, to go through the encyclopedia and find some Greek guy to be my hero, but that was the kind of thinking that always got me into trouble. I needed a normal hero.

Most of the boys were doing President Kennedy, while Emily Potter, the only other girl besides me and Irma, was doing Jackie. My parents would have killed me if I had a hero who was a Democrat, so that scratched Eleanor Roosevelt, who I liked because she was smart and out in the world and not at all afraid to say what she thought. And she was ugly. She was ugly but that didn't stop her, she didn't go hide in a corner so her looks wouldn't offend anyone.

I wanted to choose a woman, but I couldn't think of one I wanted to pattern my life on. Most of the women heroes I could think of were nurses or saints or actresses, none of which I wanted to be. I thought about Margaret Mead, because I liked the idea of studying cultures, of seeing how other people lived and thought and behaved. But I knew I could never go live in a tent in the jungle, no matter how curious I was.

In the article, there was only one woman hero mentioned and she was just some opera singer's crippled sister, who was nice and happy and brave despite the fact that she was in constant pain. She didn't really *do* anything, she just endured. Mr. Blake said that was an example of unsung heroism and suggested we look around in our own lives for unsung heroes. When I mentioned that at dinner, everyone looked at me hopefully and I wished I had never opened my big mouth. For weeks, they kept reminding me of what martyrs they were.

"The meek shall inherit the earth," Mother kept sighing, but I didn't think she believed that any more than I did. It was just something they put in the Bible to help people live with their misery. And even if it were true, it wouldn't last long—the meek would inherit the earth and the first thing they'd do was get even with all the people who'd mistreated them. Maybe this *was* the world they'd inherited; maybe Mother had been Catherine the Great and Grandmother had been some peasant she'd run over in her troika and now Grandmother was paying her back.

It was bad of me to not want an unsung hero, but I couldn't help it. I didn't want a hero who sat around smiling even though her limbs were dropping off one by one. "Oh, that's all right, don't mind me," she'd say and kind of groan softly while she leaned over to pick up the toe that had just plopped on the floor. I wanted my hero to be huge, there, out in the world, somebody *everybody* knew, somebody solid, sung, shouted, not some unsung saint who hobbled through life being an inspiration.

Grandmother was probably right. I probably was the most ungrateful girl in the world. The way Grandmother talked, you'd have thought I went around torturing people and setting cats on fire, like that creep Marvin Peabody. It was true that I was bad, but only because I didn't want to be good *enough*. I wanted to be good for all the wrong reasons—so I wouldn't get punished or so I'd get an A in Citizenship, not so I could run around healing lepers or building houses in jungles or devoting my life to Christ or being nice all the time and never saying what was real and true just because it might be upsetting. "You're heartless," Mother always said. "An iceberg," Grandmother said, "just waiting for the *Titanic*."

I wanted a hero who didn't care what people *said*. A hero who just did what she knew was right, even if it seemed selfish, even if it wasn't what everybody else thought was right, even if a million people said it's wrong, my hero could stand up and do what she needed to do, despite the clamoring. And then, when she'd done it, proved that she was right and everybody else was wrong, *my* hero would have the courage to say, *I told you so.*

They never do, in the stories. They're always gracious and magnanimous, as if it never bothered them that for twenty years people said they were crazy and treated them like dirt and laughed at them. I didn't believe that Thomas Edison, who used to work for the railroad right here in North Bay and even blew up a baggage car he was using for experiments, never once laughed and said, "Guess I showed those dumbheads."

It wasn't easy to find someone like that. Maybe hundreds of thousands of hero-type people had felt that way, but nobody came out and said it, at least not in the *Encyclopaedia Britannica.* It was easy to be gracious once the world was knocking at your door, bestowing gifts and titles and love, but what about all those years when they weren't? Back before the person was a hero and they had to endure all the name-calling and the shunning and the poverty and the ridicule, the years when they'd walk around in threadbare coats, with their scrawny children shivering in their unheated houses, while all the neighbors stared and called them kooks? I didn't believe they didn't think, I'll show *them!* How else could they keep going? How else could they keep believing in themselves while everybody else was giggling at them behind their curtains?

"That's what makes them heroes," Mother said, but what a bunch of bull-hudda. I didn't think they were doing anybody any favors by being big about it. How were people supposed to learn, if they kept plodding along, century after century, despising anyone they didn't understand, making them suffer, and then, when they finally realized the person was right all along, being forgiven like a two-year-old? Why was it that the heroes were the ones who had to be tolerant, instead of the idiots who tormented them? Wouldn't it be better for everyone if the heroes said, "Look at what stupid boobies you are!" and made the people feel bad, so they'd hang their heads in shame and think about it and then look at themselves and say, "Well, gee, maybe I *was* a booby. Maybe I shouldn't be so quick to judge."

"I don't know where you come up with these things," Mother said when I told her I was thinking of choosing Julius Caesar to be my hero. "Can't you choose someone a little more *reasonable?*"

Like who, I asked. Well, someone more recent. Someone more admirable. "After all," she said knowingly, "he had an *affair.*"

I felt it was my duty to defend him. "He was a great statesman," I said. "He was a great general. He built roads all the way to England! He developed a calendar. He's got a month named after him. He cleaned up a corrupt system of government. He practically ruled the world!"

"But what does that have to do with you?" Mother wanted to know. "You couldn't even stick out Brownies. How do you expect to rule the world?"

I told her I didn't *want* to rule the world and she wanted to know why I was choosing Julius Caesar then. Wasn't I supposed to choose someone I wanted to *be* like? I sighed and said I just wanted someone heroic to write about for stupid summer school and I couldn't think of anyone and when Mr. Blake said, "Maggie! Who is your hero?" Julius Caesar was just the first person who popped into my head. "He had fits," I told Mother. "He was an epileptic and still he was able to be an emperor."

"You're not epileptic, thank God," she said. "What does that have to do with you?"

"Nothing," I said and she said she thought I chose him to spite her, just because she wouldn't let me see "that godawful movie."

"It is not," I said and that was the truth. I'd already seen it; Ginger Moore and I sneaked in through the exit door at the Ottawa Theater and watched almost the whole thing and I didn't see what was so awful about it except Liz Taylor wore see-through togas.

Daddy thought it was funny. He talked about having been to the Coliseum and Ruthie kept interrupting to tell us her hero was Beep-Beep, the cartoon road runner. Donald said his hero was Al Kaline and Mother wanted to know why I couldn't have chosen Amelia Earhart; Amelia Earhart would have been a good hero for me.

"But she's dead!" I cried.

"So is Julius Caesar," she said.

"Yeah, but he didn't just *disappear*," I said, starting to feel all panicky and tight, as if I might burst into tears and I couldn't do that, I couldn't cry in front of her, I couldn't let her know she'd got to me. "He didn't get in his plane and crash and *disappear!*"

"That's true," Mother said, poking the ends of her corn cob with the little plastic holders. "His friends murdered him."

I was outraged. She wanted me to disappear. She wanted me to get in a plane and fly off and never return. She could put a picture of me up on the mantel and point to it when the Bridge Ladies came over. "And that," she could say, sobbing ever so lightly, "was Maggie. She went on an adventure and never came back."

It was what I'd always suspected, but I didn't expect her to be so blatant about it. Didn't she just say she thought I should choose someone I wanted to *be*? A zillion heroes in the world from which to pick and my own mother wants me to pick the one who plops in the ocean and is never heard from again.

Ruthie started crying; she thought someone was going to kill me. "Maggie's gonna be murdered in an airplane!" she blubbered. "Who will be my sister?"

"Now look what you've done," Mother said and I couldn't believe it.

"Me!? All I said was I chose Julius Caesar as my subject for a stupid paper for stupid summer school. *You're* the one who brought up Amelia Earhart!"

"And *you're* the one who brought up plane crashes!"

Donald started giggling and Ruthie began to flap her arms and Mother started to cry. "I can't do *anything* right!" she sniffled, tossing her corn on the plate and sending the butter splattering. "I can't say *anything* around here!"

Daddy thumped the table and said, "All right, all right, let's stop this caterwauling and eat."

I couldn't believe she was being so obvious about it, right in front of Daddy. And what was *he* doing, sitting there grinning and bemused, as if he didn't notice? She'd always wanted me to disappear—from the moment I was born, she wanted to be rid of me and I wasn't just making it up, I knew it. I even heard her once, talking to Mrs. Tucker on the phone and crying because she couldn't "control" me and she *admitted* it, kind of. She was talking about Grandmother, and how Grandmother used to come over and tell her what a lousy mother she was and what a lousy housekeeper she was. "I wanted to prove to her that I could be a good mother," Mother told Mrs. Tucker. "I wanted to prove to her that I wasn't like *her*." I felt sorry for her when she said that and I almost ran into the room to jump on her lap and hug her, but then her voice got all hard and nasty and she said, "But that child was uncontrollable from the day she was born. It was almost as if she was trying to make me look bad in front of Mother."

So that was how I knew. And maybe she was right, maybe it *would* be better for her if I did just disappear into some ocean. But I still wasn't going to have Amelia Earhart as a hero.

Chapter 5

WHAT a mess. Here I was, stuck in summer school with all the delinquents and dumbheads, having to write a paper about some dead emperor I didn't even like.

I looked out at the Lake, at all the sailboats skimming by with their spinnakers billowing out like gigantic balloons, and I wished I could swim across the Lake, just jump into the cool, clear blue and swim and swim until I could no longer see our beach, no longer see the shoreline, until I could look back and see only a memory of North Bay.

I would be the first person to do it—the first person ever to swim across a Great Lake! Even though I knew it was impossible—I'd never even made it past second sandbar—I thought I'd like to try it. What a glory it would be! I could be my own hero and everyone would admire me; my parents would be proud of me and I'd be forgiven. Well, if not forgiven, at least redeemed. "Oh!" they'd say when they saw me on television, exhausted but jubilant. "She wasn't crazy, she was just special."

"What makes you think you're so special?" Grandmother endlessly asked. "Who put you on that high horse?" "Just who do you think you are?" Mother would want to know, putting on her Grandmother voice. "You're heading for a fall." Even Daddy would get in on the act: "Don't start thinking you're special," he'd warn, reminding me that the party I was having was paid for out of *his* pocket.

But why *wasn't* I supposed to think I was special? I didn't get it. We were supposed to excel, and to excel is to be special, but if we weren't supposed to want to be special, how then were we supposed to excel? "Goodness is its own reward," Mother said, but what did that have to do with wanting to be special? Nothing happened when you were good; you became invisible, mute, you did what you were told and melted into everybody else and I hated that. I hated it more than getting kicked out of class for being "unruly," hated it more than the hours I spent sitting on the filthy floor in that dark old hall, counting doorknobs and getting my skirt all grimy. I hated it more than I hated being yelled at; more than I hated having to spend three hours a week with a social worker; more than I hated being banished to my room. Being good meant being placid and there was something in me that just refused to follow along like a zombie.

"You just do things to be different," Mother said, but what was so wrong with that? I thought we were *supposed* to be special, and I guessed that was OK as long as you were special in the way they wanted you to be: if you were a Champion Speller or Miss Teenage America or something. But if you weren't, watch out! They'd call you a Communist or a homo; they'd run you out of town, like poor Mr. Hilliard, who lost his job as County Clerk just because he spoke Russian. "He might be a *spy!*" everybody said, as if the Russians cared about who got married in North Bay. I knew Mr. Hilliard and he was a very nice man; whenever he'd see Goober and me out walking on the beach he'd invite us in and tell us stories about North Bay history. He lived in the last house on Beach Street, just before the coastguard property, which probably didn't help his case much. Like maybe he was keeping track of how many times the lighthouse light went around in an hour or something strategic like that.

It was dangerous to be different, at least if you were different in a way that wasn't approved by the world. I wanted to be part of the world, but I didn't want to get lost in it. I didn't want to be an indistinguishable ingredient in some cake batter, all swirled around and mixed in with the rest; I wanted to be a raisin or a walnut, always keeping my own identity even though I was part of the cake. Mother laughed when I told her that—she thought it was the silliest thing she'd ever heard. But at the same time she looked kind of sad and lost, as if she knew exactly what I meant and just didn't want to admit that being the baking soda wasn't a whole lot of fun.

I wondered what would happen if I tried to swim the Lake. It seemed as if I could do it, if I really tried, if I just kept going instead of turning back when I got tired. "Don't go past second sandbar alone," Mother always warned. "A boy from Riverside got run over by an outboard between sandbars." But I wasn't afraid. I knew my limits; I knew when to turn back, when I had just enough energy left to get back to safety. Each time I tried, I got closer and closer to third sandbar—I could feel the water growing colder as the Lake floor dipped deeply, then growing warmer again as I neared third. I'm close, I'd think and take a deep breath and drop myself straight down, like an anchor, to see if my upraised hands would feel air while my toes wriggled on the slick rocks. But it was always over my hands, too deep to continue, so I'd turn back.

"I wonder if Julius Caesar had a miserable childhood," I asked Goob, and she climbed into my lap. I suppose he did, what with his epileptic fits and all. His parents must have been beside themselves every time he flopped down on the floor and started writhing around like a hooked fish. "I just don't know what we're going to do about Julie," his mother must have moaned, pulling out her hair and rending her toga. "I can't *control* him!" "I don't know what gets into you, young man," his father probably said. "If you don't shape up we'll have to send you to Gladiator School."

I had copied all the information from the encyclopedia but I didn't know what to do with it. There were certain things that weren't very heroic about Julius; for instance, he was big on pillage and plunder and in Gaul he captured a village and then cut off everybody's hands so they couldn't raise arms against him. I thought that was kind of drastic, even for barbarians.

I looked down at my notebook, not knowing what to say. It didn't really matter; I was a delinquent, not a dumbhead, and my grade didn't even count. But everything I did had to be perfect or Margaret would have a fit. She went crazy if I so much as got an A−. She'd run out in the hall and start scratching my arms until she drew blood, to punish me for not getting it right. "Stupid, stupid, stupid," she'd say, scratching like mad, and Mr. Blake called my parents and told them there was something wrong with me. "Nonsense," Daddy said, "she's just competitive. It's a good quality to have in this world. And look at it this way, at least she doesn't scratch anyone *else.*"

My problem was I couldn't concentrate. All I had to do was take the facts from the encyclopedia and tell about Julius Caesar and why I thought he was admirable, and that was that, a cinch. But every time I tried to think about Julius

Caesar, my mind would drift off—I'd start thinking about swimming across to Canada or being the first woman governor of Michigan or catching the Pervert or marrying Rocky Colavito or something. Something that would redeem me, so I could come back to North Bay and not be hated. I liked to think of the future because it was the only hope I had.

"This is the happiest time of your life," Mother always said, and I'd want to climb up on the roof and jump off. If this was as good as it was getting, I might as well get it over with.

"Suicide is selfish," she said when I threatened to hang myself from the ceiling fan in the sunroom. "What about all the people left behind?"

"What *about* them?" I asked. "Maybe if they cared in the first place, the person wouldn't want to kill himself."

Mother said I was mean, wanting to make people suffer their whole lifetimes, wanting them to spend every day thinking, Maybe I could have done something, when the person who kills himself is dead and doesn't care about anything.

"That's the point," I told her. "They want to stop caring."

"I don't know where you get your ideas," she said. "You should be the happiest girl in North Bay and all you want to talk about is suicide."

"It's not *all* I want to talk about," I told her. "It's what we're talking about *now*."

"Well," she said, "I don't want to talk about it. It's morbid. Can't you find something positive to do?"

She turned and walked away, into the living room, to listen to the baseball game on the radio. I would have gone with her, to listen while Rocky Colavito smacked a homerun right out of Tiger Stadium, over the scoreboard and out, out, all the way to Windsor. But I couldn't. I didn't want to go crawling after her, begging for attention, so I stayed in the sunroom, watching the ceiling fan turn, thinking about how stupid I'd look, strung up from one of the blades, my neck broken and sagging, circling around over the summer dinner table while the rest of the family ate their grilled hamburgers and potato salad, the first of the season. "What a shame Maggie isn't here," Mother would say, glancing at my empty plate. "She *loves* potato salad!" And I'd circle above them, my feet swinging right over their heads, and they wouldn't even notice until Mother said, "What's that noise?" and they'd all look up and see me dangling like a wind chime. "Harumph! Maggie's hung herself from the ceiling fan again," Grandmother would say. "She's just doing it to be *different!*"

In our family, there were three reasons to do things: because you had to, because you wanted attention or because you were selfish and never thought about anybody but yourself. Everything you did had to be weighed and measured and all the possible consequences had to be considered. For instance, if I hung myself from the fan, I had to think about hurting them and making everybody feel guilty for the rest of their lifetimes and embarrassing them by making them look like a bad family and possibly ruining Donald's and Ruthie's lives, for who would want to have anything to do with someone whose sister strung herself up from a fan? No one would marry them, they'd be afraid of bad genes and it would be all my fault because I was too selfish to think about them, I only thought about my own miserable little life and how I wanted it to end. Grandmother would say it was all Mother's fault and spend the rest of her life tormenting her, giving her a double dose because I wouldn't be around to catch any of it. And if by some stroke of bad luck I didn't happen to die, I'd have to go through life with an ugly rope burn around my neck and I'd have to wear scarves all the time, or maybe even get a white rubber neck, and I'd spend the rest of my life playing bridge with Cindy and Ginger Moore and Karen Harmon and when I left they'd sigh and say, "What a shame; Maggie would have made such a wonderful wife and mother, but who would have her with that neck?"

If we were Japanese, I wouldn't have to worry about any of that; I'd just plunge a sword into my heart and nobody would think anything of it, in fact, they'd probably say, "It's sad but it was the right thing to do after having disgraced herself and her family."

I tried to kill myself after the trouble at school. I stayed home one day and took every pill in the medicine cabinet: all the aspirins, both baby and adult, all Mother's cramp medicine, all the allergy pills and even a whole box of Ex-Lax. I went back to my bedroom and lay on my bed, preparing to die. I took my Bible from under my pillow and started reading Revelation, to find out where I was going. I had barely opened the Bible when all of a sudden my ears started vibrating, as if there were some Roman gong-ringer in my head, pounding furiously. It seemed like my head was about to explode from the noise, as if ten thousand bees had built a hive in it and were buzzing crazily while the Roman went berserk with his gong. I covered my head with my pillow, but that just made the noise louder. Then my stomach began to churn and I had to throw up. I didn't want to because I knew if I did, I'd live, but I couldn't help it, those pills were coming back up and there was nothing I could do. I tried to stand, but I was too dizzy, so I rolled off my bed and crawled down the hall, into the bathroom, and started puking. It seemed like I was in there for weeks and I didn't come out until Donald came home from school and pounded on the door, screaming to Mother to make me unlock it.

Eventually, she came up and I let her in and when she saw how sick I was she felt bad for thinking I'd only been faking another bout of the Mystery Illness. Nobody knew I'd tried to kill myself, and even if they suspected, nobody said anything. One night I heard Daddy go to the medicine cabinet and shout, "Where's my Ex-Lax?" and I heard Mother say she guessed we were out and it was the oddest thing, we were out of everything all at once, and she didn't know how that could happen but she was sorry.

I didn't tell anyone and I certainly wasn't going to tell Miss Dickerson, who would have pulled a straitjacket out of the first-aid cabinet and sent me off to Lapeer. "Suicide is a cry for help," I read in one of Mother's magazines, but no it's not. At least not for me. I didn't want any help, I wanted to start over, to have a chance to do things right. "Everything I do is wrong," Mother always moaned and I knew what she meant, even if the thing that was wrong was totally inconsequential, for instance, having broccoli instead of beans with the chicken. I would have said, "Tough luck, Clarabell, if you want beans, go cook them yourself." But that would have just been what I *said*. Inside I would have been going nuts: Margaret would have been scratching like crazy and Sarah would be crying and Cotton Mather would be telling me I was going straight to hell and Katrina would be wanting to skate to Amsterdam and Trixie would be singing, "Beans, beans, the musical fruit,/ The more you eat, the more you toot," and I would have been sitting there, wanting to scream, thinking, Everything I do is wrong.

The things I did wrong were worse than serving broccoli instead of beans. I was only twelve; I had sixty or maybe even seventy years ahead of me, during which nothing good could happen to me because I'd already filled up my heart with black spots and nothing good could get in. If you start building a house and find out the foundation is rotten, you tear it down and start over. My soul was rotten and therefore I thought I should be able to kill myself and start over. It made perfect sense to me and I didn't see why suicide was such a big sin.

But I couldn't even commit suicide right. The only thing that happened was I made myself so sick I couldn't go out of the house for three days. I pretended that I really was dead, that being trapped in the house with Grandmother for three days was purgatory and on the third day, I'd wake up and be an angel, hovering over my body while it lay in bed, watching it and saying goodbye before I sailed off to heaven to wait for my new life.

But no such luck. Grandmother would barge in and stand in the doorway with her hands on her hips, glaring at me and saying, "There's nothing wrong with you that a few licks with a thick belt wouldn't cure," and the gong would start again and I'd be in so much pain I knew I had to be alive.

Chapter 6

IT was hopeless. I couldn't concentrate on Julius Caesar. I guessed it was OK, I could always do it the night before it was due. I worked best under pressure; "Last Minute Maggie," Mother called me, warning that life wouldn't always be so easy.

"C'mon, Goob," I said, packing up my things and heading home, hoping that the Bridge Ladies had finished their lunch and retired to the living room to continue their rubbers.

But they hadn't. They were still in the dining room, sitting around the table picking at their shrimp salads and drinking Bloody Marys out of Great-grandmother MacPherson's crystal goblets. "Someday, these will be yours," Mother told me and I pretended to be thrilled, because I knew it was some kind of big honor to her. Great-grandmother MacPherson had given her them, bypassing Grandmother, who she hated and blamed for her son's death. Grandmother wanted the goblets because they were some special kind of crystal and every time Mother brought them out, Grandmother would get all huffy. I thought it was hysterical.

Mrs. Tucker was talking about sending Cindy to some fancy boarding school and I could hear Mother sighing and wishing that Daddy would let her send me away to school. "I think it would be good for her," she said and Grandmother laughed.

"Yes," she said, "it would be a good idea to send Maggie away. The further the better."

She snorted and laughed and I sat on the front porch, listening to them through the screen door, hating them, wishing the bomb would drop right then and blow them all to bits, send them flying through the air like popcorn bursting from the pan.

"Now, Kay," Miss Nolan said to Grandmother, "don't tease like that. Maggie's a fine girl."

"Phooey," Grandmother said. "She's spoiled. Spoiled rotten with a capital R and it's too late to do anything about it."

I didn't want to hear any more; Grandmother would start berating Mother for spoiling me and Mother would meekly mumble something about trying. I hated Grandmother, but I had to be careful about what I said about her. "Why, your grandmother is a *wonderful* person," Mother said when I complained about Grandmother. "Everyone *adores* her!" "But *you* hate her," I said and Mother gasped, raising her hand to her neck and holding it there, as if to strangle herself if she said anything. She stared at me like I was a mutant coming to devour her, and I wanted to die, to take the words back, but it was too late, I'd said the wrong thing and now the world would fall to pieces. "Stupid! Stupid! Stupid!" Margaret screamed. "*Now* you've done it!" "I'm sorry, Mother," I said, "I didn't mean it," but she didn't hear, she'd flown off to another planet and it might be days before she came back.

I hated it when she did that. She'd just vanish. She still looked like Mother and talked like Mother and did all the standard Mother-type things, but she wasn't there. And it was all my fault. I had made her that way, by being so uncontrollable.

I sneaked round the side of the house, hoping that the door to Donald's bedroom wasn't locked, so I could get in that way. As I circled the house, I looked up at my bedroom window and Cotton Mather said, "You're such an ingrate. You have your own bedroom and still you're not satisfied. Your grandmother is right, you're spoiled rotten."

I didn't think I was spoiled, but the facts were against me. My father was the Candy King of North Bay. Robert "Sweet Is My Middle Name" Pittsfield. It was my middle name, too. "Sweet as in anything-but," as Grandmother said.

I had everything a girl could want: clothes and books and toys and games and a nice house on the beach. I even had a candy bar named after me—how many girls could say that? I supposed that was what being spoiled was all about: having everything but feeling empty inside, wanting more but never being able to get it. "Poor little rich girl, poor little rich girl," Margaret started chanting in her nasty nasal voice.

"I am not!" I protested. I hated the idea of it; I'd rather be dead than a poor little rich girl, a whiny frail little wisp of a thing, quietly sobbing in her palace while her parents flew off to the Orient for some diplomatic mission, leaving her behind with no one but the evil aunt.

Of course, we weren't really rich, not like the Sisks. We had a nice house on a nice street in a nice neighborhood, we had nice furniture and nice cars and nice doodads all over the place, and Daddy had the candy factory, but it wasn't as if he were Mr. Mars.

"What have you got to complain about?" Cotton Mather demanded. "You've got it *easy*." It was true. I thought about the migrant farmworkers who came to North Bay to pick cucumbers for the pickle factory, living in those horrible shacks, and I'd hate myself for being so ungrateful. They had a terrible life and even the kids had to work, dragging boxes out into the field to fill them with cucumbers. How could I be boo-hooing about my own life when I thought about them?

Donald's door was unlocked and I quickly crept in, making sure not to touch any of his things. He laid traps all over his room, to see if people were spying on him—pieces of paper laying in a certain way in a drawer and his covers tucked in carefully so he could tell if anyone had been looking between his mattresses for his stupid nudie magazines.

I slipped into the kitchen, motioning to Goober to be quiet. She was unbelievably smart; she not only understood everything I said to her, she could also sense what I was feeling, and she'd always leap into my lap and lick my face whenever I was sad, just to show that she, at least, loved me.

The Bridge Ladies were gabbing so loud I thought they wouldn't notice me. They were all sitting there, talking at once, with no one listening to anyone else. I wondered if they noticed, but if they did, they didn't seem to care—they just joined in, dancing around one another but never taking a partner. Miss Nolan was talking about nine irons and Mrs. Tucker was talking about wanting to get her hands on the Bicker house, now that old Earl was dead, surely Helen wouldn't keep that mausoleum for herself, and Grandmother was talking about the difficulty of getting decent seafood in North Bay. "Now in *St. Pete* . . ." she was saying. If she liked St. Pete so much, why didn't she stay there all year instead of coming up here to torment us the whole summer?

"Why doesn't she stay down there?" I asked Daddy every June, when Mother would starting turning into a robot, running around and moving all of Ruthie's stuff out of her room so Grandmother could have it. "Why does she have to live with us?"

Daddy shook his head and said it wasn't nice of me to resent Grandmother; she was an old woman and she should be with her family. Mother was her only child and we were her only grandchildren.

"But she *hates* us!" I protested. "And she especially hates *me!*"

Daddy said no, Grandmother didn't hate me, she was just an old woman and she didn't like much of anything any more.

"But she insults me all the time," I complained. "She's always telling me how terrible I am."

"Blood is thicker than water," Daddy said, but so what?

"Why can't Mother go down there?" I wondered and Daddy got all stern and even before he said anything I was ashamed. Perhaps Grandmother was right, there probably *was* something evil about a girl who would gladly send her own mother off to Florida. "And take Ruthie with you," I would have said, if I could, if Daddy wouldn't hate me for it.

"I'm sorry," I said before he had a chance to scold me. "I don't mean it."

He pulled me over to the arm of his big velvet chair and tussled my hair in that condescending way I hated. "I know you didn't, Boo," he said, "but you have to think about what you say. You hurt your mother's feelings."

Yeah, yeah, yeah. I hurt *her* feelings, I hurt Ruthie's feelings, it was all I ever did. There was something horrible about a girl like me, something horrible and cruel and evil.

"I'm sorry," I cried desperately, "I try. I really do, but sometimes I can't help myself. I just get so mad!"

"I know, Boo," he said, "but you're strong and you have to be patient with people who aren't."

"Grandmother's strong," I said. "She doesn't worry about hurting people's feelings."

Daddy sighed. Adults always sighed that way when you

43

pointed out the obvious and they couldn't explain it away with Good-Do-Bee logic. He sighed again and said, "You have to be nice, Boo."

"I don't *want* to be nice!" I shouted, pulling out of his grip. "And stop calling me *Boo*! My name is *Maggie*!"

He just laughed; he always thought it was "cute" when I got mad. "What have you got to be so angry about?" Mother always wanted to know, but I didn't know any better than she did. It didn't make any sense. What *did* I have to be angry about? Nothing. Everything was exactly as it should be. We were the perfect American family, complete with two cars, a dog and 2.5 children, if you counted Ruthie as the .5, since she was half bird anyway.

Sometimes I thought there'd been a mistake, that somewhere along the line God had got my soul mixed up with some ghetto kid's, some mean kid who threw rocks at pedestrians from the broken window of her unheated hovel in a burnt-out section of Detroit. Someone who was bad, but who at least had a *reason* for it. Someone who needed that anger just to survive and fight her way out of the slums. And the soul that belonged to the child my parents were supposed to have living with them in their lovely house on the Lake was trapped in some poor slum kid, kind and loving, the brunt of everyone's jokes because she was so good and patient and self-sacrificing and not the least bit bitter about taking baths in cold water or fighting rats for space in her bed or having to drop out of school to take care of seven squalling siblings.

". . . why, the shrimp in St. Pete," Grandmother was saying and Miss Nolan looked up and saw me sneaking into the kitchen, so I had to go into the dining room and be polite.

"Hi," I said and they all looked up and nodded while they chewed and chatted, never missing a beat.

"There's shrimp in the fridge," Mother said with forced gaiety. "Help yourself!"

"Thanks," I said and stomped back into the kitchen.

"It's quite good," she called. "If I do say so myself!"

She waited for the Bridge Ladies to shout their confirmation but they kept right on nodding and chewing and picking like a bunch of gaudy puppets and Mother looked through the door, into the kitchen, and smiled sadly at me.

It made me want to scream, it made me want to shove their plates in their faces, to rub the shrimp in their noses until they gasped and said, "Yes! Yes, it *is* good!" I wanted to jump up and down on the table until they paid attention. But I knew they wouldn't. "Maggie, get off," Mother would say, even though I was doing it for her. "You're getting sand all over the *petits fours!*"

Instead, I said I was sure it was good. "You make the best shrimp salad in the world!" I called, taking the bowl from the refrigerator and scooping some onto a plate, even though I didn't like anything with mayonnaise on it, not even shrimp. I tasted it as Mother watched hopefully.

"It's wonderful!" I shouted. "It's great!"

"Why, thank you, dear," she said and smiled happily and turned her attention back to the Bridge Ladies as I slipped the plate to Goober, who would have praised Mother's shrimp salad to high heaven, if only she could speak.

Chapter 7

"YOU are not allowed to go into the woods behind the Moores'," Mother always said but that was exactly where I was going.

Someone was "doing things" to little girls there. "What things?" I asked, but she wouldn't say. "Things" had been found in the woods—girls' underpants, scraps of clothing, mysterious "things" she wouldn't tell me about, "things" I shouldn't know about. "What things?" I'd ask again and again, but she'd put on a somber face and shake her head and say, "You're too young to know about those things." "What things? What things?" I'd beg, but she was secretive as a saint.

I had to find out. Ginger Moore and I were building a fort back there, where we'd hide and watch for the Pervert. We'd spend hours scouring the woods, searching for "things." Soup cans became chalices for midnight animal sacrifices; broken baseball bats were the weapons used to knock out kidnap victims; campfire remnants were the scenes of witches' sabbaths. We'd hide for hours under the bushes, waiting for "someone" to come by with his screaming victim, hoping she was someone we knew so we could save her and be heroes.

But no one ever came. The stories continued, the victims were always little girls from Riverside, and I came to the conclusion that bad things only happened to me and to kids from Riverside, which was the closest thing North Bay had to a slum. They were always having something dreadful happen to them: they were the ones who dived off the canal bridge and were paralyzed for life. They were the ones who went ice skating on the Lake and fell through, the ones whose bodies were found the next spring, bloated like whales, on a beach on Harsen's Island. Don't go near the swamp, they told us, that mud's like quicksand and last year a boy from Riverside sank for ever, disappeared into the muck. I wondered why they were so unlucky; wasn't it bad enough being poor? Why did they have to be the ones who threw water balloons at cars and got run over when the car went out of control? Donald and his friends threw *eggs* at cars and they never even got maimed.

Ginger Moore was the only friend I had left. It was a miracle she stuck with me, especially after what happened last winter, when Cindy and her gang attacked her, but she did and I was grateful. What happened was this: it was before Christmas, and we'd been walking home from school, taking the short cut through the swamp behind the Donaldsons'. I knew something was up. During recess Cindy had nudged me and said, "We've got a surprise for Ginger Moore." She giggled in that mad-scientist way and I knew it was a surprise of the unpleasant sort, but I did nothing to prevent it. I could have. I could have told Ginger to walk another way; I could have called my mother and asked her to pick us up; I could have warned Ginger not to go with Cindy and that crowd. I could have prevented it but I didn't because I wanted to see what it was, what they had planned, what they were going to do to her.

It was wrong. Wrong, wrong, wrong with a capital W and bad to let it happen. I just stood there and watched while they held Ginger to a tree stump and Cindy made a snowball while Karen Harmon ripped open Ginger's parka. Cindy chopped the snowball in half, smushing both halves on Ginger's chest, and Pauline Quinlan stuck maraschino cherries in the center of each. They all went into convulsions, and Cindy started chanting, "Falsies! Falsies! Ginger Moore wears falsies!"

I stood there, hating myself for watching and not protecting Ginger, but I was afraid, afraid of what they'd do to me if I stood up for her. Until that moment, I had thought of myself as brave and bold, but watching those girls torment poor Ginger made me realize what a coward I really was.

"Stop it!" I shouted, but it was too late. It was over. The other girls ran away, giggling and shrieking, and Ginger just sat there, looking blank and lost, with the snow breasts stuck on her sweater like Christmas-tree ornaments.

I went over and wiped the grotesque balls away, but it was too late. Ginger looked at me without saying a word and we walked home in silence. I wanted to get down on my knees and beg for her forgiveness; I wanted to chase after those girls and tell them off, tell them how cruel they'd been and that I didn't want to have anything to do with them any more. But I knew I wouldn't. "Coward!" Margaret shouted. "Craven!" Cotton Mather sneered, and they were right. I was a yellow-belly, standing back, doing nothing, and I suddenly realized that it wasn't Ginger's forgiveness I wanted—she'd forget all about it in two days—but my own forgiveness, which I would never give to myself. I was horrible and weak, vile, the kind of person who could close her eyes and let a world be destroyed and then when it was over, open them wide in disbelief and say, "How could this have happened? I didn't see a thing!"

But that was last year and now it was as if nothing had happened. Ginger had long since made it up with Cindy and her gang and at Cindy's pyjama party it was Karen Harmon who got attacked, with Ginger joining right in, holding down Karen's arms while the other girls pulled open her pyjama top.

I didn't understand it, even though it was perfectly clear. Cindy was cruel to Ginger; Ginger attacked Karen and Karen would undoubtedly take out her rage on someone else. Once it was done, once the rage was set free, it was over and everything was supposed to go back to normal. But for me, it never did. I couldn't forget. I would always see the look of horror on Ginger's face when Karen was holding her arms and Cindy was coming at her with those snow breasts, and even though what they did wasn't the worst thing in the world, I didn't think that mattered. What mattered was the terror Ginger felt when she was being attacked, not knowing what was coming, not knowing what they'd do, and when they just smacked those stupid snowballs on her it must have been a relief and it was easy for her to forgive them because it hadn't been as bad as it could have been.

I was always secretly grateful that it wasn't happening to me, but I knew that someday I'd get mine; someday it would be my turn to have them come at me like a bunch of banshees and no one would help because why should they? I'd take it; I'd see that slitty look in their eyes and I'd know it was coming and I'd quickly turn myself off, make myself fly away and then they could do whatever they wanted to my body.

"Let's get Maggie," they'd say. That was always how it started, "Let's get Ginger or Karen or Pauline." There didn't need to be a reason; it was usually a whim, and who knew how it started? There was no way to protect yourself from it because it could be anything—I could show up at school in a dress Karen had coveted and she'd run to Cindy and say, "Let's get Maggie," and they'd attack me, drag me into the woods and rip holes in the dress and Karen would be happy, free, and the next day she'd invite me over to her house for ice cream. And I would go, because that was the way it worked. I'd go to her house and eat her ice cream and it would be as if nothing had happened. No apologies, no accusations, no discussions, just a bowl of Neapolitan with a glass of milk.

Chapter 8

GINGER Moore had been crying.

"What's the matter?" I asked but she wouldn't say; she just wiped her nose and got up off her porch step and followed Goober and me into the woods.

Ginger was always crying and that was because her mother was crazy. She'd waltz around the neighborhood in nothing but a mink coat, "visiting" people, sprawling out on the living-room davenports, holding the mink tightly against her chest with one hand while easing the other along the back of the davenport like a furry snake. "Ah'm nekkid," she'd drawl and Mother would stare at her in dismay while Daddy blushed and I'd shriek with laughter. I always thought it was some kind of joke, that she really did have *some*thing, her bathing suit perhaps, on underneath.

Mrs. Moore was the whitest woman on earth, whiter than white; if she were any whiter she'd be invisible. She stayed in the house all day, being pale and fragile, and never came down to the beach to watch us swim, or played bridge with the other ladies, or even gardened in her own yard. She only ventured out at night, always in her mink, even in the middle of summer.

"Are you sure you're OK?" I asked Ginger and she nodded, crawling into our fort, and I didn't press it. Offering comfort is a delicate business and I knew that there were times when I wanted it and other times when I would have murdered anyone who tried to give it to me, so I let it rest and pulled my surprise from under the branches.

"What is it?" Ginger asked in wonder, taking the little metal container and examining it.

I beamed. "I found it behind the Bensons'," I told her and she gasped—I'd gone into the woods *alone!* Why not? I wasn't afraid of the Pervert. If he got me, I'd just turn myself off, I'd just click the switch and escape to my safe place and whatever he did wouldn't matter because I wouldn't be there. I'd close my eyes and feel my body getting all hard and rigid, like a mannequin in Peterson's window, a fake kid. I'd open my eyes and I'd be blind; I'd stare straight ahead and see nothing. I'd put on my mean look, my You-Can't-Get-to-Me look, and once that was in place I'd flick the switch and fly off. I'd watch. I'd know everything that happened but it wouldn't be real because *I* wasn't real. I was nothing but beautiful blue, blending into the sky, the Lake, and that girl, that hard little rubber girl with the staring eyes and the mean look—she wasn't real, either. She was just a punching bag, a phoney, a storefront dummy and they never knew they were hurting nothing.

I never told anyone about my ability to escape. If they knew, they'd find a way to prevent me from doing it, to keep me inside so I'd have to feel things. They'd plug me up, stuff up all the holes and I'd never be able to get out again.

"Do you think it's his?" Ginger asked. "What do you think he used it for?"

I shrugged. "Mother uses them to keep casseroles warm when she has a buffet," I said. "I guess maybe he was cooking something."

"Toes!" Ginger screeched ecstatically. "He was probably boiling some little girl's toes!"

"The favored appetizer of Perverts," I said like a TV announcer, "a rare delicacy!"

"Marinated toes!" Ginger squealed.

"Toe à la King!"

"Toe-na noodle casserole!"

We shrieked and screeched and Ginger had to put her hand between her legs to keep from wetting her pants. She laughed so hard her face turned pink and when she laughed like that, so that the color came to her face and her eyes sparkled with tears, she was beautiful. Usually she was scrawny and pale, nearly as white as her mother, and when they first moved to the neighborhood, everybody said she was an albino, what with her mass of long stick-straight white hair and her skin whiter than eggshells, white as ice, not a color but a lack of it. "Albino aliens!" Tom Ditwell declared and dared anyone to go into their lair. They didn't call him Ditbrain for nothing.

Ginger tossed the container on our pile of Evidence and took two sandwiches from a paper bag. "I bet I know who it is," she said. "I bet it's Marvin Peabody."

I said I didn't think so. Marvin Peabody was the biggest creep in the world and a sicko to boot, but all his sickness was on the outside, for all the world to see, and that wasn't the way it was with Perverts. The thing about a Pervert was, it could be anybody. Somebody you'd never suspect, somebody nice on the outside but ugly and warped inside.

"It's like being a werewolf," I told Ginger. The Pervert probably had a perfectly normal life and was respected and well-liked and a Pillar of the Community and most of the time he was just a regular person, somebody's father, and then WHAM! He'd be overwhelmed by moon-rays or something and he'd be turned inside-out and he couldn't help himself, he'd be in a trance and he'd have this insatiable urge to do terrible things to little girls, because they were young and pure and innocent and he'd have to crush that innocence, blot it out, he'd have to stomp on it, as if it were a June bug, because when he was inside-out, everything that was good seemed bad.

"You've been watching too many horror movies," Ginger said. "That's the stupidest thing I've ever heard. *People* don't turn inside-out, only mutants."

And it doesn't have to be a man, I went on, but she didn't want to hear it.

"No woman could be a Pervert," she declared. "It's physically impossible."

But no it wasn't. And she didn't have to be a Spinster or a Lesbian. She could be a regular woman, a mother, who was usually loving and soft and pliant and kind, the perfect mother for plopping your head into her lap and sinking into safety, but boy, when those moon-rays got her, watch out!

I thought we should start looking for high-heel tracks, but Ginger said I was crazy.

"How do *you* know?" she said. "What makes *you* such an expert on Perverts?"

"I don't know," I said and I started to get that panicky feeling, that feeling that I was doing something wrong. My heart started pumping like Goober's tail on the carpet, thwack, thwack, thwack, faster and faster until I thought it would leap out of my chest and splot down right there on our pile of Evidence. I should have kept my mouth shut; now I was going to get it, God was going to punish me, He was going to poke me with His prickly thunderbolts until I took it all back, until I screamed, "I'm sorry, I'm sorry, I'm making it all up, I don't know anything about Perverts. Of course no woman could ever be a Pervert, except maybe a Nazi war criminal, but never a normal woman, never a mother!"

"If you say one more word about lady Perverts," Ginger threatened, "I'm not going to play Pervert with you any more."

Pervert was the sex game we played sometimes; we'd hide in our fort and take off all our clothes and Ginger would be the Pervert and I'd be the Victim, and she'd make me open my legs and she'd look inside me and then she'd hold my legs down and put a stick up me and say stuff like, "You are my captive," and I'd float off to that world where I was blue and wait for my other parts to take over. Margaret would get mad that I always played the Victim, and Cotton Mather would have a fit. "Dirty! Filthy! Sinners!" he'd blather, so horrified he could hardly shout. "Hell and Damnation!" Trixie kind of liked it, which scared me and made me think maybe I *was* crazy. And a couple of times, Peggy appeared, just her eyes, just staring, so scared and pathetic I'd get scared myself and start screaming for Ginger to stop and then Peggy's eyes would disappear.

"Let's go look for Evidence," Ginger suggested and we crawled out of the fort and started searching for "things."

"Are you going to be in the Parade?" she asked and I shook my head. She should have known better than to ask; of course I wasn't going to be in the Parade, I was an Outcast. Most of the time Ginger was pretty good about it. She never asked what happened and she never acted like I was crazy and she didn't wrinkle up her nose when I walked by, as if I had kooties. Not that anyone else *did*, but the way they looked at me it felt as if they wanted to, as if they wanted to hold their noses and say, "P. U. ! It's Pittsfield!"

"I'm going to be a squaw on Cindy's float," Ginger said and I nearly had a heart attack.

"WHAT!?" I shouted. "How *could* you?" How could she betray me by joining Cindy and her squaws, how could she do that to me?

She shrugged. "I want to be in the Parade," she said, "and Cindy's the only one who asked me."

Oh, great. Just what North Bay needed—an albino squaw.

"I'm sure she'd let you be on it, if you wanted," Ginger said and my mouth dropped open a mile. Sure, she'd let me be on it, because if she didn't her mother would murder her. "Why, just because Maggie's in a little trouble," Mrs. Tucker would say, "that doesn't mean you should shun her." But I would never ask Cindy to let me be one of her stupid squaws—I'd rather throw myself down the cement-plant smokestack than go crawling to Cindy for a place on her float.

I looked at Ginger, who was bent over, searching through some wild rhubarb. Maybe it was a set-up. Maybe she was supposed to lure me to Cindy's garage so they could "get" me. Maybe my turn had come and Ginger was paying me back for just standing there, watching, while they went after her.

"You're *paranoid*," Donald always said; it was his favorite word. "You're *paranoid*," he'd say when Mother cried over the broccoli. "You're *paranoid*," he'd say when Ruthie would fly off to Birdland. Everybody was *paranoid*. He thought it was because the Russians had infiltrated Canada and were sending thought-waves across the Lake to make us turn on each other so they could come over and pick up the pieces after we blew ourselves to bits.

"I thought you were my friend!" I cried, the tears starting to form behind my eyes. My throat was getting all tight and I knew if I didn't get out of there, I'd start crying, and it was against my rules to cry in public.

"I *am* your friend," Ginger insisted. "I just want to be in the Parade!" She jumped out of the rhubarb and came towards me, but I held out my arm—Don't come near me, I thought, and Goober growled at her.

"Maggie, Jeez," she said, "don't get so upset!"

But it was too late, I was already upset—my best friend, my *only* friend left in the world, was deserting me and telling me not to get upset about it, but what else could I be?

"I hate you!" I cried, but my throat was so tight from holding back the sobs that the words just came out like little peeps, little Ruthie bird-sounds.

I had to get out of there. I had to get away from Ginger before Sarah took over and started wringing her hands and crying and saying stupid stuff like, "I'm sorry! I'm sorry! I didn't mean to get mad, don't desert me, I'm sorry, it's all my fault!"

"I hate you!" I peeped again and ran further into the woods, towards the Bensons'.

Chapter 9

"WELL, now I've done it," I told Goob as we hid in the rhododendron bushes behind the Bensons', "I've lost my only friend."

Goober wriggled her way onto my lap, as if to say, "You'll always have me." Why couldn't people be more like dogs, I wondered. They always loved you no matter what and even if you got mad at them, if they'd been on the beach rolling around in dead fish and then wanted to crawl all over you and you pushed them away and said, "Yuck! Go away!" they'd just go lie down in a corner and watch you and as soon as you were nice again, they'd be jumping up and down and as happy as ever. Why couldn't people be like that? People always pretended they forgave you, but they never did. They just stored it up and the first time you did something wrong, they'd dig it out of the filing cabinet and wave it in your face and say, "You're *always* mean and nasty, remember that time you spat on me when we were two?"

I was more mad at myself than at Ginger. "You idiot," Mar-

garet said. "Now *every*body hates you." I was mostly mad because Ginger and I were going to go to the Parade together
and watch it from the roof of the bank building, where her
father had his law office. We could have stood up there, giggling and making fun of Cindy and her squaws, but it was no
fun going alone. Who could I make jokes to? Besides, if I
went downtown by myself, everybody would say, "There's
that Maggie Pittsfield. No one will be friends with her," and
the awful thing about it was that they would be right.

It was getting late and cold and I supposed I should go
home, but I didn't want to. I wondered what would happen if
I stayed there all night. I doubted that the Pervert would
come, because the whole point of his being there was to trap
little girls and since there weren't any little girls in the woods
at night, there was no reason for him to be around.

I could hear mothers calling their kids—Mrs. Keller calling for Rick's little sister Casey and Mrs. Peterson Jr. calling
for Kevin. I baby-sat for both of them, not overnighters, just
if their parents were going out for dinner or something.
Mother couldn't get over it: "They must *like* you!" she'd say in
wonder as she handed me a message from Mrs. Peterson Jr.
or Dr. Keller. But getting kids to like me was easy; the trick
was not trying to control them, not trying to strap them into
the rules their parents handed over to me, along with the
keys to the house. We'd become friends, conspirators, staying up way past their bedtime and eating popcorn and playing the one last game or reading the one more story their
parents would never allow. So when I'd look at the clock, the
kids would be as amazed as I was and skip docilely off to
their beds while I stayed up to watch the horror movie on
TV or write in my diary, and we were all perfectly happy.
Sometimes I worried about breaking the parents' rules,
thinking they'd find out and brand me a Bad Influence and

ban me from baby-sitting circles, but I suspected they already knew and that they didn't really care—it was worth it to them to get out of the house without their kids kicking and screaming and clutching their evening gowns.

"Casey! Casey!" Mrs. Keller called and I felt kind of sad. My mother never called for me and I suspected she didn't care if I came home or not, even though when I did come in the door she'd make a big deal out of it and say, "Where have *you* been? I've been worried *sick!*" Maybe she was embarrassed to go running around the neighborhood calling for me, because she thought it made her look like she hadn't trained me well enough to be home on time.

"C'mon, Goob," I said and we sneaked out of the bushes to see if the coast was clear. I disliked having to sneak around the Bensons'. First you had to hope their monster St. Bernard wasn't out—that dog would attack anything that moved and he'd already bitten half the boys in the neighborhood. Getting past Hans was an endurance test the boys imposed upon one another and having a bite scar was a badge of honor in Edison Woods. Then you had to hope Clara wasn't out. Clara was the Bensons' daughter and there was something wrong with her. She was as old as my mother and the Bensons kept her shut up most of the time, or let her walk to the beach and back with her "companion," who was as crazy-looking as Clara, only she wore a uniform.

Clara had red hair and big green eyes that never looked at anything. They were always darting around in their sockets, like hummingbirds, hovering but never lighting. She was tall and skinny and Mother said she'd been quite beautiful as a girl and that she'd been normal all through high school. "What happened to her?" I asked, but Mother didn't know or wouldn't tell; she just said Clara came back from her first semester at college and never went out of the house alone again. "Didn't you ask?" I asked. "Didn't you want to find out? She was your *friend*, wasn't she?" Mother said she'd tried to see Clara, but the Bensons wouldn't let her in. "They were probably ashamed," she said, as if that explained everything. "I assume they felt it was their fault."

That was the first time I realized that if I went crazy, not only would I suffer from the craziness itself, but also from the guilt of having made my parents feel bad. They'd have to build a wall round the house and get a bunch of Dobermans to keep out the neighborhood kids who would come to gape and taunt. I vowed to be more diligent about hiding my crazy streak—I hated the idea of being walled in and never being able to make a move without some white-shoed attendant following me around like my conscience. Everyone would whisper when I shuffled by like a zombie and mothers would tell their children I had been perfectly normal, in fact I had baby-sat for them when they were little, and then all of a sudden something snapped and I had to be walled in with my parents for ever.

"What happened to Miss Benson?" I asked Wally, who knew everything. Wally had the corner store, up on St. Joseph Avenue, and he was my fourth favorite person in North Bay. "I don't know, Toots," he said, shaking his head. "She was a nice girl, but she was flighty. Kind of like Blanche DuBois." I wanted to know who Blanche DuBois was and Wally said she was some crazy southern belle. "You mean like Mrs. Moore?" I asked and Wally laughed so hard he spat his coffee all over the counter. "She never looked you in the eye," he said as he wiped up his spit. "Remember this, Margarita: there's something wrong with somebody who won't look you in the eye."

I asked him if he meant there was something wrong as in the person was bad, or something wrong as in something bad *happened* to them and he said that was a good question. He thought about it for a minute and then said, "Wrong as in they're hiding something. There's something they don't want you to know and I guess it doesn't matter much whether it's something they did or something that was done to them. Whatever it is, it's not exactly *right*."

Luckily, Hans wasn't out so I climbed over the Bensons' fence and crept along it, hoping nobody was looking out the window. Mr. Benson would come out with a rake if he saw kids sneaking around, and chase after them as if they were stray cats. "Go on, get out of here!" he'd shout and the kids would shriek with fright and joy. Then he'd kind of shuffle back to the house, looking old and defeated. I felt sorry for him, but not as sorry as I felt for Clara. You were always supposed to feel sorry for the parents rather than the children; after all, the parents worked and slaved and sacrificed and bent over backwards and for what? "You, you ingrate!" they'd shout. "And what have you done for *me*? Nothing! A big fat zero! After all I've done for you, you go crazy and now I can't go out of my house without a rake!" In the movies, it was always the parents who were good and kind and sweet and self-sacrificing and it was the children who were evil and who tormented their poor, bewildered parents for no reason other than sheer wickedness. I hated those stupid movies. They gave kids a bad name.

Goober had already crossed the Bensons' yard and I could hear her at their gate, barking for me to hurry up. Tom Ditwell said one night he saw Clara come out and run about in the yard, screeching like a hawk, circling around in some weird Indian dance. That was when the rumor started that the Bensons belonged to a cult and had sacrificed Clara to get in. It was a stupid rumor, but the kids liked it because it was scary. It didn't help that the house itself was spooky: a two-story dark pointy house with tiny leaded windows with shutters on the inside that really closed. It had been surrounded by big old elms, but they all got sawed down, like ours, when the Dutch Elm disease hit North Bay and turned Edison Woods into Edison Shrubs. The Bensons replaced their trees with fat, prickly bushes that grew right outside the windows. We used to dare each other to sneak up to the house and peek in, to see if Clara was running around in a black cloak and a pointed hat, and I guess that was why the Bensons got Hans.

There was music coming from their house, some kind of opera, and I ran the last few yards, hopped over the fence and jumped down. Safe! I looked back and there was Clara, standing in the window, waving at me as if I'd just been to tea. I waved back, sadly, and thought about how lonely she must be, stuck in that dark house with only her parents and that fat old nurse, who was about as friendly as Hans. I wished I could talk to her—I'd ask her what happened, straight out, and I bet she'd tell me. She'd probably just been waiting, all these years, for an opportunity to tell someone what happened but no one ever asked because they were afraid to hear. I wasn't afraid. I wasn't afraid to ask and I wasn't afraid to hear. I was only afraid of being locked up for the rest of my life.

Chapter 10

DADDY wasn't home yet, which meant it wasn't six o'clock. We had dinner every night at precisely six and the only one who was ever allowed to be late was Donald, and only on days when he had baseball practice. We didn't wait for him; we'd start at six and Mother would keep his dinner warm in the oven. I missed him when he wasn't at dinner; I adored Donald and I could usually rely on him to stick up for me, even if it was only by rolling his eyes and kicking me under the table. Sometimes we'd be through eating by the time he got home and I always felt sorry for him, having to sit at the table all alone to eat his crusty dinner, as if he were being punished, but Daddy said, "We eat at six and we don't wait for anyone." Even when we had company we started at six and if they were late we started without them, even though Mother cried and said it was rude and what would our guests think?

"They'll think they should have been on time," Daddy would say, chuckling as if it were the funniest joke in the world. He thought it was an insult to be late; it showed a lack of respect and it appeared as if you thought your time was more valuable than the other person's. Once, when I was ten, we were going on a trip up north and I ran over to Ginger Moore's to say goodbye and I guess I took too long because when I ran back, Daddy had already pulled out of the driveway and was rounding the corner. I could see Mother, straining around, looking out the side window, and I chased after them, feeling like a fool, shouting and waving my arms and pretty near crying. "Robert! Robert!" Mother was shouting. "Stop the car! What will the neighbors think?" He stopped and waited for me to run up before he answered: "They'll think Maggie must have done something really bad to get left behind," he said, giggling, thinking it was the funniest thing since whoopee cushions. "We were going to leave without you," he announced as I climbed in and shoved Ruthie over. Mother said no, they wouldn't really have left without me, but I suspected they would have, if I'd been two seconds later. They would have driven off to Sault Ste. Marie and left me all alone in the house without even Goober, who was imprisoned in some horrid kennel.

When I got home, Mother was standing in the kitchen, looking at the pile of dishes left over from the Bridge Ladies' lunch. Ruthie was sitting at the table, ready for her dinner, even though the place settings weren't on yet. That meant we were having chicken and I'd have to sit next to her while she gobbled up the wings, getting covered in grease and making horrible slobbering noises. "You cannibal," I'd say. "How can you eat your own kind?" but she'd just squawk and flap her arms and keep right on eating.

I didn't know why she was the only one who didn't have to have table manners. If Donald or I so much as crunched our lettuce too loudly we'd get sent from the table, but

Ruthie was allowed to peck at her plate, like some kid bobbing for apples in a barrel, and it drove me crazy.

"I can't *stand* it!" I'd always say. "I can't *stand* all her *noise!*" and she'd start crying, saying, "I can't *help* it! I can't *help* it!" but of course she could and they just let her get away with it because she was a psychopath.

She really was. She was only eight years old and yet she'd taught herself how to stuff birds. She had a regular little taxidermy shop in the garage and all the neighborhood kids would bring us any dead birds they found lying around and Ruthie would take them into the garage and start operating with a Projecto knife, cutting the stiff body open and pulling out its insides and then filling it up with cotton balls or something. She made Daddy take home movies of it and then she'd show them, along with her bird movies. "That's the epiglottis," she'd say as we sat around the living room with the drapes drawn, looking at bird guts, and Daddy would say, "I had a real hard time holding the camera for that one."

She kept dead birds in the freezer and sometimes I'd come running home from the beach to get a Popsicle or something and I'd reach in the freezer and pull out a sparrow. It was really sick.

"I'm hungry, Maggie," Ruthie said. "Hurry up and set the table."

"Set it yourself," I said and she started to blubber and Mother moaned and said, "Margaret Sweet Pittsfield, can you *never* be pleasant? You're in the house five seconds and you're already being mean to your sister."

"Yeah," Ruthie sniffled, "if you were nice to me, I'd be normal."

I doubted it, but still I felt guilty. I always felt guilty; it was a way of life for me, but it didn't change my behavior. If I had to feel guilty no matter what I did, I might as well do what I wanted.

"You *have* to set the table," Ruthie said, sitting there like some sultan's wife. "It's your job."

"I just walked in the door!" I shouted. "Can I at least go to the bathroom? Can I take a second to go to the bathroom?"

"Hurry up," Mother said. "Your father will be home any minute and he'll have a fit if the table's not set."

Let him, I thought, let him have a fit. He acted like it would be the end of the world if dinner wasn't steaming in his face at precisely six o'clock, as if the whole universe would be set off balance if we weren't in our places, saying grace, as if God would leave without us if we weren't on time.

I locked myself in the bathroom and sat on the toilet seat, wondering what I'd do now that I was friendless. "Nice work, dumbo," Margaret said and Cotton Mather wanted me to drown myself in the tub. "Now, now," Sarah said, "it's not as bad as all that."

When Sarah wasn't busy crying or whining or wringing her hands, she liked to be a Good-Do-Bee. She was always saying things like "Forgive and forget," and "Turn the other cheek" and all that blessed-are-the-meek stuff.

"Count your blessings," she said and I had four. The first was Goober, who was everything a friend should be. She listened to me without interrupting and never threatened or teased or turned on me, like real people do. Ginger used to have a dog, a silly hotdog named Fritz who she called Bean. "Bean as in human bean," she said and it was true, dogs were more human than people, or at least they were all the things that everybody kept telling us we were supposed to be but never were themselves. Loyal. Trustworthy. Devoted. Loving. Protective. Playful. That goofball Fritz was the best thing in Ginger's life—he'd get on his back and scoot across

the floor like a swimmer doing the backstroke. "Swim, Fritz!"
we'd say and down he'd plop, with the corners of his muzzle
turned up as if he were laughing too. Too bad Mrs. Moore
had him gassed. He pooped in her bedroom once and that
was his death sentence.

My second blessing was the Lake. I knew how lucky I was
to live in a house right on the Lake, to have my very own
beach and a place to run to. In the summer I was in the Lake
more than I was out of it. I had a bright yellow raft with a
clear plastic view-hole in the pillow, and I'd lie on it and
paddle out, looking straight down to the rocks below and
watching the fish swim by. Last summer a foreign freighter
had brought some lampreys into the Lake, stuck on the bottom of the boat like barnacles. They attacked the fish and all
summer long hundreds of dead fish washed up along the
shore, making it reek like a sewer. Goober loved it—she
couldn't wait to get out of the house and run down to the
beach and roll around in all those slimy silver bodies. I guess
the eels must have frozen to death during the winter, or gone
back to the ocean, where they belonged, because we didn't
have a problem any more. "Nature takes care of itself,"
Mother said.

My third blessing was my family. I should have put them
first on my list, and it would have hurt their feelings to be
third, even though they didn't *know* I had a list. They gave
me a nice place to live and they were nice to all my friends
and weren't too embarrassing, for parents. They were the
kind of parents you could go places with and while they
might not be outstanding in any way, at least you didn't have
to worry that they'd end up dancing with a lampshade on
their head or getting up to sing with the band or falling
down the stairs dead drunk, like Cindy's ex-dad used to do.
We were all terrified of Mr. Tucker—he used to come home

and if Cindy wasn't there, he'd come tearing out of the house screaming for her and drag her all the way home by her ponytail. It made me understand why Cindy was so mean, but understanding it didn't mean I had to like it.

For my fourth blessing I counted all my bodily parts, which were all in place, except my tonsils and adenoids, and all in good working order. I was healthy and at least I didn't have a wooden leg, like Wilma Bosniak. Wilma was in Donald's class and had got polio and had to have her leg removed. The fake one wasn't really wood, it was plastic, kind of skin-toned, and it was hooked onto her body with metal clasps and I thought it must have hurt like hell. Wilma lived in a stone house on Beach Street and I remembered playing with her when I was little, before she got polio. I remembered the wonderful playhouse she had in her basement: a miniature, kid-sized house with little chairs and tables and cupboards and everything. I wanted to go live there and Mother nearly had a fit when Mrs. Bosniak told her I'd asked if I could move in. I loved Wilma's basement—it was so safe down there and whenever we'd have tornado warnings, I'd sit huddled with everyone in the downstairs closet, wishing I was safe over at Wilma's, but of course I would never desert my family, let them get sucked up in the funnel while I stayed safe and sound in Wilma's playhouse.

We didn't have a basement. We just had a little utility room, which wasn't even underground and would have been no use whatsoever in a tornado, much less an atomic blast. A few years ago, when the Prittles put in a bombshelter, Daddy had a contractor come over to build one for us, too, but we were too close to the beach and there was nothing under our house but sand. In a way, I was glad. Before we knew we couldn't have one, I'd lie awake all night, wondering who I'd invite to come hide with us if we got attacked. It was horrible; some people would have to get left out and I thought it would be our fault for not letting them in and I just hated the idea of it. Now that I was friendless, it wouldn't be such a problem, but I was still glad we didn't have a bombshelter. I think I'd rather have been blown to bits than spend ten years in a windowless room with my family.

When Wilma got polio, we weren't allowed to play with her any more; she was quarantined away in her house and she was never the same after that. She kept herself apart, out of shame, I guessed, and fear of being ridiculed and rejected. She couldn't bear to have anyone watch her walk, and I could hardly blame her. It wasn't very pretty. Her fake leg had a kind of metal hinge at the knee, but either it didn't work or Wilma couldn't figure out how to use it, because she'd keep it straight and stiff and every time she took a step, she'd move her good leg forward and then swing the fake leg around, from the hip, like a sack of potatoes. When the bell rang to change classes, everyone would run through the halls and then when the second bell rang, you could hear Wilma slowly thudding down the hall like Frankenstein's monster. I thought she should just forget the fake leg and get crutches. Then she could move faster and she could just jab anyone who dared to make fun of her.

So, when I thought about Wilma, hiding herself away because of her leg, or about the poor people in Riverside, living in their rickety houses with their grey scrubby lawns and their kids who were always falling through the ice or getting sucked into the swamp, or about Mrs. Moore and Cindy's ex-dad, I thought I must be the luckiest girl in the world and it was a sin I wasn't happy, grateful, cheerful, kind and normal.

"You are the most morbid child in the world," Mother always said, but look who was talking. The woman who would shut herself up in her bedroom, crying for a week, because she couldn't cook broccoli.

"Margaret Sweet Pittsfield!" Mother shouted up the stairs. "You get down here this instant! The table needs to be set!"

"I'm coming, I'm coming," I growled, hating the poor table and its important needs, as if it would crumble into dust and die of shame and loneliness if it weren't set exactly right and exactly on time. "I'm *coming!*"

Chapter 11

RUTHIE was sitting in her place, waiting. Her patience was unbelievable—she'd spend hours out in the garage, just looking at those bird corpses, drawing them over and over again until she got them perfect. I was exactly the opposite. I'd try something once and if I didn't get it right, it got tossed and I was running to something else. "Miss Perpetual Motion," Mother called me, saying if I didn't slow down I'd have a heart attack.

I grabbed the blue and white woven place mats from the cupboard. They were my favorite ones, the ones Mother brought back from Portugal when she flew over to meet Daddy, leaving us with that horrid Mrs. Jolly. She was one of those devout people who thought playing cards was sinful. "Mrs. Anything-But," I called her and even Grandmother had to laugh.

"Remember Mrs. Jolly?" I asked Ruthie as I shoved a place mat in front of her. She giggled as she moved aside, not the least bit offended by my pushing into her territory. Unbe-

lievable! If someone tried to barge into my territory, I'd re-
fuse to budge, I'd make myself into a pillar, I'd push them
right back out. But not Ruthie. She was the most docile and
placid child in the world and I guessed it just wasn't that
important to her; she'd rather have me speak nicely to her
than preserve her boundaries.

"You and Cindy got all silly," she said, holding her chubby
hand over her mouth and laughing. "Mrs. Jolly was going to
call the police."

"What?" Mother cried. "What's all this about the police?"

"It's nothing, Mother," I said. "She's just talking about the
time Cindy and I drank that cider."

"Oh," Mother said, giggling herself. They'd arrived home
from their trip and we had all run out to greet them, to help
them with their luggage, jumping up and down with joy,
while Mrs. Jolly stood in the doorway, grim as a hatchet,
waiting to chop me to pieces. "Ruthie and Donald were angels," she said without even a how-was-your-trip? "But Margaret was scandalous."

"Scandalous." That was a first. Sometimes I thought I was
doing my siblings a favor just by being alive; they always
seemed like angels, compared to me, and Donald especially
got away with murder because no matter how bad he was or
how much trouble he got into, it was never as bad as something I'd just done. Besides, he was a boy and boys were
expected to have a certain amount of badness, otherwise
they could turn out to be sissies.

"Well, I guess that incident will keep you away from the
cider from now on," Mother said, but cider was for babies. I
already drank the hard stuff, sometimes; I had a jar of Mother's Scotch hidden under the eaves and every once in a while
I'd mix it with Coke and sit there all night, thinking about
being the first woman governor of Michigan or the first

woman astronaut or the first person to swim the Lake. I liked getting dizzy and then having the world get kind of lopsided and hazy and it was the only time when all my parts seemed to be one. Or maybe they disappeared. I didn't know, all I knew was that when I was hiding under the eaves, drinking that Scotch, I felt comfortable with myself and there were no voices screeching and clamoring and telling me how rotten I was. I felt peaceful and calm and I liked that, even if I had to pay for it the next day, when as soon as I'd wake up, Cotton Mather would start pounding his pulpit and telling me I was beyond salvation and I was going to turn into an alcoholic, even though I was only twelve.

It wasn't exactly fun, not like that first time, with Cindy. We'd been up in my bedroom, hiding in the Black Hole and reading horror comic books and making gum-wrapper chains and drinking the cider I'd brought up from the garage. We didn't realize it was hard, not at first, but it tasted different, all fizzy and tart, as if someone had put carbonated water in the jug. After a few glasses, when we started screeching and laughing so hard we couldn't breathe, we figured it out, but by then we were having too much fun to stop. Suddenly, everything was hilarious and bright and sparkling and the world seemed so easy, so wonderful and all our little troubles seemed so absurdly insignificant. Who cared if I was crazy, who cared if Cindy's ex-dad had sneaked in their house and stolen all the silverware?

We put on records and danced around; we ran into my parents' room and pulled down Mother's hat boxes and we even grabbed Ruthie and dragged her into my room and dressed her up like a witch, painting her face with Mother's make-up so she looked like a ghoul from the comic books. She was in heaven—she didn't understand why Cindy and I were so happy, but it didn't matter to her, she just wanted to be happy too, and she laughed and acted as silly as we did. We ordered pizzas to be sent to all the neighbors houses and then watched out the window, nearly suffocating with laughter, as the pizza boy stood there with his box while Mr. Ditwell shouted and pointed and slammed the door in his face. Everything was outrageously funny, even Mrs. Jolly lumbering up the stairs shouting, "What's going on up there?"

She barged into my room and stood there like a hangman, scowling at our glee. She gasped when she saw the horror comic books lying around, and when she saw Ruthie painted up like a monster, she nearly keeled over. "Torturers!" she shouted. "Devils!" We fell on the floor laughing and Ruthie tried to stand up for us, crying streaks of red and black, saying, "We're *playing!* We're having *fun!*"

"You've been drinking!" Mrs. Jolly gasped when she saw the empty jug. "You're *drunk!*"

Cindy and I rolled on the floor, laughing so hard it hurt, shouting, "Stop! Stop! You're killing me!" and Mrs. Jolly grabbed Cindy and yanked her up. "*You!*" she said menacingly. "Go home. And don't ever come back here!" She pushed her out of my room and although Cindy was shaken, she managed to stand behind Mrs. Jolly and pretend to kick her in the butt. "Don't! Don't!" I tried to say; I knew I'd really get it if I kept laughing, but I couldn't help it—there was Cindy, all red-faced and messy, standing behind Mrs. Jolly's flat, skinny butt, making faces and pretending to sniff, rolling her eyes and holding her nose.

"You!" Mrs. Jolly said, pointing a skinny finger at me. "You are not leaving this house until your parents come home."

"What about school?" I said. "You can't make me stay home from school. You can't make me do anything."

She started coming at me and I wasn't happy any more; I got up on my knees and backed into the corner and thought, if she touches me, I'll kill her. I looked around for a weapon but there was nothing with which I could bludgeon her. She kept coming closer and closer and I wanted to scream, to run, to be a tank and roll right over her, squashing her into my ink-stained carpet, making her into just another grey blob that Mother couldn't get out. Save me, save me, save me, I thought and then suddenly Margaret appeared, fierce and vicious, and shouted, "Don't you TOUCH me!" in a voice so shrill and powerful Mrs. Jolly stopped, still as a stone. Cindy and Ruthie stood in the doorway, their eyes popping out like bubble gum, while Mrs. Jolly started to shake with rage as she backed up.

"She said I was evil," I told Mother as I plopped the silverware on the table, letting it rattle loudly and watching while Mother's back stiffened.

"Who did, dear?" she asked, turning to smile, as if clattering silverware didn't bother her in the least.

"Mrs. Anything-But," I said. "She said I was a fiend from hell."

Mother shrugged. That was all in the past and better forgotten.

"I liked it when you were silly," Ruthie said, looking up at me adoringly. "You were nice to me."

Her eyes were shining with innocent, devoted love and I felt terrible—how could I be so mean to someone who was so sweet and vulnerable? If I so much as smiled at her, she beamed with happiness; she'd instantly forget all the times I made her cry or gave her the evil eye. I wanted to reach out and tousle her billowy curls, to grab her and throw her up in the air like a baby, to cuddle her like a doll, as I did when she was little. She was so trusting, so willing—I knew she'd trust me to catch her, just like a baby, just like a little kid, always thinking someone would be there to catch you if they tossed you up.

I looked down at her, grinning up at me as if I were some kind of hero, and I suddenly felt this horrible rage wash over me, like a blood-red tidal wave, pounding down and sucking me in, pulling me deeper and deeper down to the bottom of the Lake. Ruthie wasn't Ruthie any more, she was turning into a baby, a tiny baby, and all I could see were her eyes, staring at me, and I wanted to shake that baby, make it miserable, hurt it, give it what it deserved. Better get used to it, better get used to it, a foggy voice in the back of my head was saying, better learn to like it.

I shook my head, trying to make the baby go away, to shake the voice out, but they wouldn't go. The baby just kept staring at me, just eyes, so innocent and full of trust, and the rage kept churning like a disease and my insides were burning and I wanted to start pulling my skin off, to get away from myself, from the fury, to get *out*.

Ruthie's hand was tugging at my arm. "Peggy! Peggy!" she said and I nearly smacked her.

"What did you call me?" I screamed, scaring her and making her cry.

"Maggie," she sobbed, "I called you Maggie! It's your *name!*"

I looked down at her, crying as if her little heart was broken, and I thought maybe everybody was right, maybe I *was* crazy, maybe I *was* nuts, maybe they *should* tie me up in a straitjacket and haul me off to Lapeer, where I couldn't do damage to anyone but myself.

"I'm sorry, Ruthie," I said, "I didn't mean to scare you."

She looked up at me hopefully. "I wish you were silly all the time," she said, and so did I.

Chapter 12

RUTHIE always said grace. She was the religious one in the family; she believed fervently and cried for my soul when I said damn. "You're going to hell!" she'd sob and I'd say so what, what difference did it make to her where I went after I was dead? "You're my sister!" she'd weep. "I don't want you to suffer for ever!"

I wasn't looking *forward* to it, but I didn't think it was anything to cry about. At least, I told her, I'd finally find a place where I fit in.

"No talking about hell at the dinner table," Daddy declared and we sat silently, waiting to be served.

"Mrs. Benson called," Mother said as Daddy handed me a plate piled high with chicken and scalloped potatoes. "She said you were sneaking around their yard again."

"I wasn't 'sneaking around.' I was cutting *through*."

"That's Private Property," Daddy said sternly. "You have got to develop a sense of respect for other people's property. How would you like it if people used your bedroom as a short cut?"

I shrugged. It wasn't the same, but there was no use arguing about it. Besides, they could burst into my room any time they wanted—Mother wouldn't let me put a lock on the door: "What if the house burned down?" she wanted to know. "How could we get you out?" But really she just didn't want me to have any privacy. I'd be in the middle of dressing and suddenly Mother would open the door and leer at my half-naked body and say, "My, my, you're already quite a woman," and I'd want to die of shame.

"So!" Mother said cheerfully. "We had a wonderful game today!"

"What do you mean, wonderful?" Grandmother snapped. "We *lost!*"

"Yes, but we had a lovely time."

"Maybe *you* had a 'lovely time,'" Grandmother growled, "but I don't consider losing 'lovely.' I want to *win.* And we would have, if you'd learn to bid, for Chrissakes."

Ruthie gasped and Daddy grunted. "Now, Kay," he said, "this is dinner."

Daddy was the only one who could shut Grandmother up. She seemed to be scared of him, but I don't know why. She wasn't scared of anyone else, but maybe she worried that he'd kick her out or that we'd move during the winter and not tell her where we were. She'd done that once, to Mother. Mother came home from college and when she got to her house, there was another family living in it. Grandmother had just upped and moved and not bothered to tell Mother. "I forgot," she said when Mother finally found her, and Mother didn't do anything. I would have killed her. I would have strangled her, I would have spat in her face and said, "I don't want to live with *you,* anyway, you old hag."

"Let's have a peaceful meal," Daddy said and I rolled my eyes and Ruthie gobbled her chicken wings, already greased up like a body builder. It was disgusting. Mother went on and on, talking about no trump and finesses, and I wished Donald were home, so I'd have someone to kick under the table and make faces at. "Dinner is family time," Daddy always said but I never felt part of it. It was supposed to be the time during which we discussed family problems and told each other about our lives, but I didn't want them to know anything about me.

"How's Julius Caesar?" Daddy asked and I shrugged. I told him I wasn't sure I wanted him to be my hero.

"Why not?" he asked, chuckling as if I were getting ready to say something hilarious. "What's wrong with Caesar?"

"He starved out the rebels in Gaul and then had the survivors' hands chopped off," I said.

"Margaret!" Mother gasped. "We're having *dinner!*"

"Well, he *asked,*" I protested, and Mother sighed and wanted to know why I couldn't have a nice hero, like Betsy Ross.

"Betsy Ross!" I cried, rolling my eyes. "Oh, *please!* All she did was *sew!*"

"Yes, but she sewed the flag that kept our soldiers going," Mother said. "She did something very important, just by staying home and sewing. 'They also serve who only stand and wait.'"

"Blah," I said.

"Miss Nonconformist," Grandmother said scornfully. "I'm surprised she didn't choose Attila the Hun. He'd be right up her alley."

"No, he's right up *yours,*" I said and Mother turned cement-colored and Grandmother said, "Why, you little sh . . ."

"Now, Kay," Daddy said, trying to stop her before she said shit, as if our pure little ears had never heard it before. Shit, shit, shit, Donald and I said it all the time; on family trips, we'd ride in the way-back of the station wagon and look for "sh" words on the billboards and the one who got the most shits by the end of the trip, won. We'd crouch down, with only the tips of our heads and our eyes peeking over the back window, and laugh and laugh until Mother said, "Just *what* are you two doing back there?"

"She needs to be taught a lesson," Grandmother said. "If she were mine . . ."

But I wasn't. I wasn't hers or anyone else's and she couldn't touch me. I wasn't a piece of property, some shell on her Florida beach, that she could crunch under her heel or toss back in the ocean or cover with shellac and set on a glass-topped table.

"She's nothing but trouble with a capital I," she said, and Daddy said, "Leave her alone, she's just a kid."

"Kid, my derrière," she retorted.

"Come on, come on, let's have some peace around here," Daddy said. "What do you all say to the Dairy Queen?"

"Bawk! Bawk! Bawk!" Ruthie squawked, indicating her approval and Mother thought it was a wonderful idea, the Dairy Queen would be lovely.

"What do you say, Boo?" Daddy asked.

"I'm on a diet," I said and they all hooted.

"Whoever heard of such a thing?" Mother wanted to know. "A twelve-year-old on a diet?" But I wasn't going. I wouldn't be caught dead at the Dairy Queen with my *family*.

Mother knew what I was thinking and she looked sad and I felt bad for hurting her feelings. I hated it when they did that; when they'd sit around looking like lost souls, making me feel like a monster because I didn't want to pile in the car and sing songs and drive through town looking like some stupid TV family, happy and carefree and clean. How could I expect her to understand when she was so dutiful herself— after all, for four months a year, she had Grandmother clinging to her back like a snarling hump.

"Oh, Maggie, please come," Mother said and I wanted to

scream. Why couldn't they just leave me alone? I'd said I didn't want to go, so why couldn't they just say "OK" and *go*; why did they have to stand at the door, looking back at me as if they'd never see me again? It made me so mad—if I went with them, I'd hate myself for giving in and doing something I didn't want to do just because someone's stupid feelings would be hurt otherwise; but if I didn't go, I'd hate myself for hurting their feelings.

Grandmother was already in the car, shouting, "Let's get this show on the road!"

"Are you sure you won't change your mind?" Mother asked, kind of pleadingly, and I wondered if she wanted me along so Grandmother would torment me, rather than *her*.

"No," I said and went upstairs.

Chapter 13

MY bedroom was long and narrow, with a little dressing room at the end that Mother called the Black Hole. At either end of the Black Hole were storage spaces directly under the sloping roof of the main part of the house, which we called "under the eaves." The one on the left-hand side of the room overlooked the sunroom and there was a crack in the floor where I could see down and hear what people were saying if they talked loud enough.

On nights when I was banished from the dinner table, I'd hide there and wait for them to move out into the sunroom to watch TV. Donald would be first, then Ruthie would follow, sucking on her stuffed zebra and climbing up on the end of the couch to rock. I hated that couch. I wouldn't even sit on it; I'd rather have sat on the floor or the footstool than on that dumb couch. It was stupid and ugly and I wished Mother would get rid of it, toss it out on trash day and replace it with something nice, something soft and smooth and comfortable, something to sink into, something covered with pink flowers, not that scratchy brown tweedy stuff. It hurt. It hurt to sit on it, it hurt to look at it, I hated it and I wished Goober would pee all over it so Mother would have to get a new one.

Ruthie didn't seem to mind. She'd put her hands on the armrest and start rocking back and forth, back and forth, for hours. She'd done it all her life, practically since the day Mother brought her home from the hospital. "Sweet dreams," Mother used to say as Donald and I trudged upstairs after *I Love Lucy,* and I'd lie in my dreamy white four-poster bed, listening to Ruthie across the hall, pounding her crib against the wall with an impossible fury. "How can a two-year-old have that much strength?" I had asked Mother and she said it was normal for children to rock in their cribs. "Rock, yes," I said, "not break through the wall like a tank!" Hoo-WHOP! Hoo-WHOP! Hoo-WHOP! Hours and hours of it—rhythmic, monotonous pounding like cannibal drums, Hoo-WHOP! "I think you'd better get her checked," I told Mother. "I think there's something wrong with her." But Mother said that was nonsense, of course there was nothing wrong with her, how could there be? She was just a child, a perfectly well-adjusted child and I ought to be ashamed of myself for suggesting anything to the contrary.

Daddy would come next. He'd sit in his big armchair in front of the TV and watch his "programs" and then he'd sneak away to his den to "work." Mother would come last, carrying her drink in one hand and a coffee cup in the other. She'd sit down on her corner of the couch and pull her feet up under her butt, like a college girl sitting in a dorm room, and take out her knitting and sit there, smoking and drinking and knitting, all at the same time. When Grandmother was here, she'd stomp out like a general and plop herself down in the best seat and start complaining. I wished the crack in the floor was big enough to stick a peashooter through it; I would have loved to shoot slobbery spitballs at Grandmother's fat head.

I'd sit up in my hiding place, listening to them talk about how bad I was. That was how I found out they were going to send me away if I got into any more trouble. "I just don't know what to *do* with her," Mother told Daddy after what happened with Mr. Howard. "I can't *control* her." Daddy was sure I'd outgrow it; he thought I'd outgrow everything. "Robert, this is serious!" Mother insisted. "This is the Last Straw!" "All right, all right," Daddy said. "Let's see how she does in summer school and worry about the rest later."

Grandmother said I was the Black Sheep of the family. Youth Gone Awry. The Bad Seed. What I needed, according to Mr. Blake, was discipline. What I needed, according to Mother, was to be brought down a few notches, to be swept off my High Horse. What I needed, according to Daddy, was to sow my Wild Oats; I'd be fine, he said, in a few years when I outgrew all this acting-out nonsense. What I needed, according to Grandmother, was an exorcist.

"You'll get yours," Grandmother always threatened and she'd have a conniption fit when I'd say, "Get my *what?*" "You'll see, Miss Flip," she'd say and they'd all sit there staring gloomily off into space while Grandmother predicted my journey to hell in a handbasket.

I'd go to reform-school movies to see what was in store for me. I'd end up a criminal. I'd be locked up in a cage, where I belonged, and no one would care. I was a Threat to Society, not fit for the companionship of nice people. I'd be sent to jail and forced to make license plates and I'd get into fights with tough girls from Detroit, who hid sharpened screwdrivers in their ratted hair. I'd have a record and my whole life would be in black and white and it would be no-

Rebecca Stowe

body's fault but my own. I'd marry a mobster and get kidnapped by some rival gang and they'd send bits of my body
back in the ransom notes—bit by bit, they'd send me back
until there was nothing left but my torso to toss in a garbage
dump. My husband, Rocco, wouldn't pay the ransom, of
course—he'd just toss out my body parts as they arrived,
giving them to one of his henchmen to stick in the inciner-
ator. Once he got to know me, he'd hate me, just like everybody else, and he'd be glad to get rid of me, even if it was
only piece by piece.

Eventually, Mother would put down her knitting and
carry Ruthie upstairs, never even bothering to knock on my
door to see if I was still alive. What if I'd fallen out of bed
and cracked my head against the spindly foot and was lying
there bleeding to death?

She'd go back downstairs and try to talk, but Daddy
would be lost in his own world. "I'm watching my program,
Marion," he'd say, or, "I'm in the middle of an article." He'd
get up and go into his den and hang up the NO TRESPASSING
sign and Mother would sit there, all alone, knitting in the
dark.

Clickety, clickety, click, the sharp needles would go,
glinting in the light from the lamp, clickety, click, and it
drove me crazy. I couldn't stand the sound of them; I couldn't
even bear to be in the same room with Mother when she was
knitting. "Put those things AWAY!" I'd shout and she'd wonder what on earth was the matter with me, but I couldn't help
it, I had some kind of phobia and I couldn't stand those
needles. I'd get all nervous and get that teeth-chattery feeling and I'd say, "I can't STAND it!" and Mother would point a
needle at me and say, "You stop that nonsense *right this instant!*"
shaking that blue metal needle at me, and I'd want to pull off
my skin and start screaming and I'd cover my eyes and run
from the room.

"I just don't know what gets into her," she'd say to Daddy.
"She's some sort of maniac." But no I wasn't. I just couldn't
stand those needles.

She wanted to teach me how to knit, but I wouldn't learn.
I wouldn't go near those needles; I hated them, I hated everything about them, I hated everything sharp and pointy and
it was a good thing I wasn't Chinese, because how would I
eat?

I didn't know why she had to knit anyway; she never *made*
anything. She just sat there, knitting and purling and clicking and at the end of the night, she'd rip out all the stitches
and start all over. "Your grandmother is the knitter in the
family," Mother would say. But not any more; she gave it up
when I was little and I didn't see why Mother had to follow
in her footsteps, as if it were some great destiny to be ful-
filled, especially since Mother wasn't any *good* at it.

"Why do you have to knit all the time?" I asked her and
she shrugged, as if she didn't know either. It was just something she did, mechanically, like a robot, clickety, clickety,
click, endlessly knitting the same green banner. "It gives me
something to do with my hands," she'd say and I'd get so mad
Margaret would come roaring out, furious as a bull, and
shout, "Don't SAY that! Shut up! Shut up! Shut up!"

Mother would start crying and I'd run upstairs and hide
under the eaves and Margaret would disappear and I'd feel
terrible for making Mother cry. I'd watch her through the
crack as she sat there, alone and sad, and I'd wish she'd get
up and *do* something. "Go to the piano," I'd urge her telepath-
ically. "Get up and play 'Stormy Weather,'" but she wouldn't.
She'd just sit there, with the needles clicking like beetles on
the window screen and it made me so upset I wanted to die.

Chapter 14

MOTHER had a box full of mementoes tucked in the corner of the eaves, next to the Christmas ornaments, and sometimes I'd empty it out and look through our history while I was snooping on them. She had all our old report cards and all the Mother's Day cards we'd made over the years and hundreds of photographs of us all, looking so happy I couldn't believe it was us.

I loved to look at the old photographs, especially the ones with me in them. I suppose that was bad of me, and proved I was stuck on myself or something, but I couldn't help it, the pictures with me in them were just more interesting. Every stage of my life was there, snapped by the camera and stamped on a glossy piece of paper, and it made me feel safe to see myself at three, standing with Donald in front of the house in our matching cowboy and cowgirl outfits, or standing on a chair in front of the kitchen counter, mixing a birthday cake for Mother. The pictures reminded me that I was real; that I always had been real and always would be real, and that I wasn't just some girl someone had made up.

Whenever I started feeling crazy, I'd crawl under the eaves and take out the pictures and look at myself, sitting on the couch holding Ruthie in my arms as if she were a new toy. I looked so pleased and happy and proud of my baby sister, how could it be that I was evil and made her so crazy she thought she was a bird? There was nothing evil in any of the photographs, not one of them, and I thought that if I were truly a demon it would certainly show; in at least one photo there would be a hint of horns sprouting from my head or a black X outlined on my forehead or something. But instead of looking evil, I looked kind of sweet, and that was comforting, if surprising.

The only pictures I wouldn't look at were my baby pictures. Once I found one that had "Peggy, 15 months" written on the back and it upset me so much I tore it in a zillion pieces and flushed it down the toilet. They used to try to call me Peggy, but I wouldn't let them. "My name is Maggie," I told them and I had a fit if anyone called me anything else. I didn't even like it that Daddy called me Boo and I was completely insulted when he came up with the candy bars for us and he named Donald's Donniebar and Ruthie's Ruthette and mine he called Boobar. "Boobar the elephant," the kids at school teased, but luckily I wasn't fat, so I didn't take it to heart.

Mother's scrapbook was in the box with the photos, with all the clippings from when she was a singer. She could have been a star. She'd sung with a big band in Detroit, Jimmy B and his Trumpets Three, and there was even a poster with a drawing of Mother looking young and sultry. She looked like me, only pretty. She was good: "Jimmy B's new songbird, Marion MacPherson, is the sweetest-sounding lark to fly into the Motor City," one of the clips said, but she gave it all up when Grandmother got sick and Mother had to come back to North Bay to take care of her.

Sick, my foot. Grandmother was only sick when it suited her and I think she just faked it, just to make sure Mother didn't get a life of her own. I think Grandmother was jealous; she couldn't bear the idea of anyone being better than her and she wanted to make sure Mother didn't fly too high.

And it wasn't just Mother. Grandmother couldn't stand it if anyone escaped from North Bay and went on to something in the Big World. I think she was even secretly glad when Miss Nolan came back, with that white blob of rubber sitting in the middle of her face, as if somebody had hit her with half a deviled egg. Grandmother blamed Miss Nolan's nose on her dreams—she'd wanted to be a professional golfer and had spent every day, summer in North Bay and winter in Florida, playing golf. "Getting her nose fried instead of doing something *useful*," Grandmother said. "She wanted to be Somebody and look what happened to her."

Mother thought Miss Nolan could have made it if it hadn't been for the cancer that ate up her nose. She'd got as far as the LPGA tournament in 1952 and came in eleventh, shooting 318 for 72 holes. "*I* can do that," Daddy teased her, "in only *nine* holes."

She had given up her life to golf, single-mindedly pursuing her dream, turning down the suitors who chased after her and the chances to be, as Grandmother said, what she was *supposed* to be, not what she *wanted* to be. And now it was too late for any of those other things. "Elvira Nolan is one of the loveliest human beings I have ever known," Mother said. "But let's face facts. Who would want to wake up next to that nose?"

Grandmother never said, "That's what you get for flying too high," but the words were always there, floating above her head like a little thought-balloon. She didn't want anybody to have anything and I thought she was the nastiest woman in the world, but Daddy said I had to be understanding. "She's had a hard life, Boo," he said but I didn't care, I didn't think that entitled her to begrudge other people their lives.

Grandmother's life was hard because her husband died when Mother was only two. Great-grandmother Mac-Pherson took care of Grandmother and Mother, even though she hated Grandmother, giving them money and a place to live, but Grandmother never got remarried and she said it was Mother's fault, that nobody wanted to marry her because she had a child clinging to her skirts. I felt more sorry for Mother than Grandmother—it was bad enough, having Grandmother around at all, but it would be terrible if I didn't have my family to act as buffers sometimes. Poor Mother had had to be alone with her, with no father to protect her, and that must have been awful.

Mother never sang any more, except at Christmas when she'd get a little tipsy and all nostalgic; we'd be singing Christmas carols and she'd open up the seat of the piano bench and pull out her old sheet music and sing the songs she sang with the band and it was wonderful, she had such a sweet, high voice, and I thought she should make a comeback, but she wouldn't even try.

She wanted me to be a singer, like her, but fat chance. First of all, I couldn't carry a tune in a bucket, as Grandmother pointed out every time she heard me singing. Last year, when I sang in the Talent Show, I could see Grandmother in the audience, with her nose all scrunched up like she was sitting on a pile of turds, leaning over and whispering to Mother, probably saying "Get the hook" or something. Poor Mother was sitting there, white as a picket fence, looking like she was dying of shame, and I wanted to run off the stage and flush my head down the toilet, but what could I do? I was already up there, with my head full of lather and the music playing "I'm Gonna Wash That Man Right Outta My Hair," so instead of trying to sound like Mary Martin, I just concentrated on the motions, doing a goofy take-off and turning it into a comedy, deliberately missing the notes and acting like I'd got soap in my eyes. Everybody was laughing like crazy and when I finished Miss Hildegarde told me it was the best number in the show and everybody congratulated me, except Grandmother, who wanted to know how I could get up there and make a moron of myself. And Mother, who was so stunned all she could say was, "But Maggie, you have such a *sweet* voice when you want to, why did you *do* that?"

But I didn't have a sweet voice. *She* did. My voice, even at its best, was loud and rough. I used to be a first soprano, but after I had my tonsils out my voice changed and I got demoted to the altos.

Thank God Daddy wasn't there. He said he had to work, but we all knew he was taking the opportunity to stay home and play with his soldiers. It would have hurt my feelings if I'd thought I was any good, but since I already knew I was a charlatan, it was just as well he wasn't there to see me, just in case I fell on my face.

That was the last time I appeared in the Talent Show. I didn't even audition this year because I was in disgrace and anyway, I would have been booed off the stage before I even got started because everybody would say, "There's that Pittsfield girl, the one who started all the trouble," and they'd all get up out of their seats and walk out, not wanting to be in the same gymnasium as me.

I heard the sunroom door open and then Grandmother's voice as she stomped into the house, and I felt sad and angry. I wished they'd stayed away longer, I wished they'd go to a

Dairy Queen on Mars and come back in a few years, after I'd had time to live out my life and redeem myself.

Goober read my thoughts, as always, and got up from the pile of dirty clothes on which she'd been sleeping and crawled in under the eaves to get in my lap. I could feel Sarah coming, wanting to have a good cry, and I didn't even fight it. Let her cry, I thought as I lay down with my head resting against Mother's box of mementoes, and she did.

Chapter 15

WHEN I woke up, it was already morning and my neck was killing me from having used a box as a pillow all night, and that put me in a worse mood than usual. I was a real grouch in the morning and it was the only bad thing about myself that none of my parts yelled at me for, and that was only because none of *them* wanted to face the day, either.

Grandmother was sitting at the breakfast-room table, scowling at Ruthie as she leaned over her cereal and lapped the milk like a dog.

"There's something wrong with *this* one, too," Grandmother said. "It must come from Robert's side of the family."

I hid behind the louvred doors between the breakfast room and the dining room, motioning to Donald to be quiet, and slowly extended my arm, waving it in the air like a snake. I made hissing noises as I reached out for Grandmother.

"Eeeek!" she screeched, jumping from her chair and patting her hair. "Oh, you vile child!"

Donald started laughing so hard he got the hiccoughs and Grandmother stomped away from the table.

"Marion, what are you raising here?" she demanded. "A family or a *zoo*?"

"What's *she* doing here?" I muttered to Donald. "I thought she was going to Detroit with Miss Nolan."

"It's none of your business, Miss Impudence," Grandmother said as Mother brought me a glass of orange juice. Grandmother stood in the middle of the kitchen, glaring at me and picking her red fingernails, and I wished I could wave a magic wand and make her disappear, send her off to some alien universe where people were even meaner than she was and where they'd chase her around all day, saying, "What makes you think you're so special, Miss Smarty-Pants?"

I wouldn't even mind if she were dead. That was evil of me, but I couldn't help it. She'd lived long enough; she'd had a lot of happy years tormenting Mother and then me. I didn't see what was so wrong with wishing she'd just go to sleep and never wake up. Everybody dies someday and she was almost seventy, that was a long time to live, why couldn't she move over and make room for someone else?

I knew I'd pay for having such bad thoughts—Cotton Mather was already climbing up on his pulpit, getting ready to attack, to threaten me with hell and worse, but I couldn't stop the thoughts from coming. They were only thoughts, there was nothing in the Bible about Thou Shalt Not Wish Thy Grandmother Dead, in fact there wasn't even anything about *honoring* your stupid grandmother, it was only your father and mother, and I at least tried to do that, even if I wasn't always real good at it.

"God knows everything you think," Cotton Mather said, "and you're going to suffer for your evil thoughts."

"Oh, leave me ALONE!" I yelled and Donald nearly jumped from his chair. "I didn't do anything! I didn't do anything!" he shouted and Mother wanted to know what in God's name was going on and Ruthie started crying and

Grandmother just stood there, picking at those devil nails of hers and glaring.

"Don't you have to go to school or something?" she asked and I pushed my chair back from the table and grabbed my notebook.

"It's none of *your* business!" I screamed and fled out the sunroom door while Mother called after me, "Maggie! Your breakfast! People will think I don't *feed* you!"

Goober came bounding out behind me and even though we weren't supposed to let our dogs follow us to school, I always did because I liked to have her waiting for me when I came out. They kind of relaxed the rules a little in summer school; they even let girls wear shorts, which suited me just fine because I always wore them anyway, even in regular school, under my skirt so nobody could look up.

Goober and I ran towards the Sisks'. I wanted to stop at the shrine and confess my thoughts to their Virgin Mary and maybe that way I could get through the day without being tormented by the Puritan. It probably *was* bad of me to be so insolent, but I felt it was my duty—nobody else stood up to Grandmother and *some*body had to. I was already the Black Sheep, and I guess in a way it was expected of me. Nobody else did anything; Ruthie would just start flapping off to Bird-land and Donald would ignore her. For some reason, she left him alone and I figured it was because he was a boy. How wonderful to be a boy, to be left alone, to be allowed to miss dinner, to wear dirty clothes and not have anyone chase you round the house with a stupid lace dress saying, "But don't you want to look like a *lady?*" To be independent, to go places alone, to be strong enough to protect yourself—if I were a boy, no one would ever touch me. If I were a boy, I could be whatever I wanted to be, I could be myself, I could live my life and nobody would be nagging me, "*Ladies* don't

do this and *ladies* don't do that, don't you want to be a *lady*?"
No! No, I didn't want to be a lady; I didn't want to be powerless; I didn't want to learn to like anything I didn't like.

Tom Ditwell was just coming out of his house as I passed
and I sighed. Now I'd be stuck walking to school with him
and I wouldn't be able to go and confess.

Tom was the only kid in summer school for being both a
delinquent *and* a dumbhead. I didn't think he was as stupid as
he seemed; he could memorize anything he heard in about
fifteen seconds, and once you showed him something, he
had it down instantly. He remembered by heart every story
that his mother had read to him as a kid. I didn't think that
was very dumb, but facts were facts and Tom was in the sixth
grade and couldn't read. My theory was that he had hysterical blindness that only occurred when he tried to read, probably from when he was little and was in Catholic school and
the nuns beat the alphabet into him.

"Hey, Maggie!" he called. "Wait up!"

He jumped over the fence and came running over.

"Have you finished your hero paper yet?" he asked and I
shook my head and told him I was thinking of changing
heroes but I didn't have a new one.

"Can I have your old one if you don't want him?" he asked
and I felt sorry for him—he really *was* stupid if he thought
Mr. Blake would believe he wrote a paper on Julius Caesar.

"No," I said, but he looked so heartbroken I offered to do
someone else for him. "I'll do Rocky Colavito for you," I said
and he threw his books in the air and tried to hug me but I
pulled away.

"On top of everything else, you're a cheat," Cotton
Mather accused, but it wasn't cheating. I'd get the information and write the paper and then Tom would memorize it
and then pretend to read it in class and it would be as if he

wrote it himself, because he'd *know* it and what difference would it make who got the information out of the library?

"Are you going to be in the Parade?" he asked and I sighed. The Parade, the Parade, the Parade, it was all anybody could talk about, as if it were a big deal, as if we didn't have one *every* year.

"No," I said and Tom said he was riding on his dad's float.

"I'm going to be a sparkplug," he said proudly and he got all offended when I laughed, even though I didn't mean to hurt his feelings, I just thought it was funny.

"Isn't your dad having a float?" he asked and I shook my head. Daddy never had a float in the Parade. Instead, he had a booth at the end of the parade route and gave out candy bars to the marchers as they drooped in. "They're tired," he explained. "They need a little pep-me-up."

"You could probably ride with us," Tom said. "I think we still need a cylinder."

I said no thanks. Even if I were entirely covered by a costume, people would know it was me, standing under the DIT-WELL AUTO PARTS banner and they'd hiss and boo and throw rotten tomatoes at me and it would ruin Tom's day.

We were getting close to McKinley and I winced as the pain shot up my butt. It happened every day; as soon as I reached the school grounds the pain would start and I'd spend the whole morning in agony. It started right after the trouble. I didn't tell anyone about it; I just let it happen, thinking it must be some kind of punishment. It only happened at school and even though it was horrible, as if there were a sharp piece of glass embedded in my butt, I endured it. It wasn't too bad when I was standing up, but when I sat down I thought I'd die from the pain. I learned to lower myself into my seat slowly, keeping my back and legs as much in line as possible, so I ended up half-sitting, half-sprawled in the chair and my teachers would say, "Maggie! Sit up straight!" and I'd pull myself up, nearly puking from the pain, and sit the way they wanted me to.

As soon as the last bell rang, I'd dart from my seat and the pain would be gone. But then something worse started to happen. I couldn't use the bathrooms at McKinley any more; I was too terrified to go in them, so I'd walk home, alone, making sure to be alone, hiding out till everyone had left, and then halfway home I'd pee my pants. It would drip down my legs, hot and shameful, and I'd wish I were dead. I never cried, not through any of it—not through the pain shrieking up my butt like a knife, not through the shame of peeing all over myself like a baby. I just thought it was what I had to live through.

I'd come home and take off my soaked underpants and hide them under the eaves, along with the ones I'd stained when I was having my period. I refused to wear one of those awful napkins, I just bled and then hid the evidence. "You go through more underpants than anyone I know," Mother used to say. "What on earth happens to them?" and I'd shrug and say maybe someone stole them out of my locker at the Golf Club or something.

"You stay here," I told Goober when we got to the baseball diamond. "I'll be back soon."

She wagged her tail and lay down, perfectly still, and I always wondered if she stayed like that all morning, or if she got up and sniffed around and visited other dogs and then came back in time to lie down and wait for me.

I only had to take classes in the morning. I guess they figured making me get up early all summer was punishment enough. It was too boring to believe—rehashing all the things we'd already learned, over and over again until I wanted to jump up and scream, "Tippecanoe and Tyler, too, you dummies!" It was bad of me to be impatient with the others; after all, they were there because they'd failed, not because they were disciplinary problems.

I didn't give Mr. Blake much trouble. I'd just sit there, squirming like a worm, waiting for the morning to be over. Once a week Miss Dickerson came and I'd have to go see her first thing in the morning and spend an hour with her, sitting in the first-aid room while she tried to get me to talk. "Name, rank and serial number; name, rank and serial number," I'd chant as I trudged down the hall to her cubicle. That was all I was giving her.

In a way, I wished I could talk to her. It would be such a relief to talk to someone besides Goober and the Sisks' Virgin Mary, but I couldn't trust her. I couldn't trust anyone. She wouldn't believe me anyway, and if she did, what could she do? She'd say I was making it all up and then she'd go to my parents and I'd get punished all over again for breaking the unbreakable no-squeal rule, and no one would protect me, so why bother?

"How is your summer?" Miss Dickerson wanted to know and I shrugged. How did she expect it to be?

"What are you doing?" she asked and I said, "Going to school."

"Well, you must be doing something besides going to school," she suggested. She was always so calm, I could never believe it. I didn't trust it, nobody could be that calm. Inside, she must have wanted to take her briefcase and start batting me over the head with it.

"I'm making a fort in the woods," I said and she said that sounded like fun.

"It is," I told her. "I'm hunting for something."

She raised her eyebrows. "What?" she wanted to know and I said it was a surprise.

"How are your classes?" she asked, trying to wheedle information out of me.

"They make my butt hurt."

"Oh?" she said, trying to be nonchalant. "Why is that?"

I sighed. It was *her* job to figure those things out. Why did she need me to tell her?

"Because it reminds me of Mr. Howard, that's why."

"And why would thinking of Mr. Howard make your butt hurt?" she asked but that was all I was saying. I'd said too much already. Besides, I didn't know. Why *did* thinking about Mr. Howard make my butt hurt, why not my head or my arm, which was the part of my body that had got bruised, why not my leg or my foot? And what was it about the trouble that made me unable to pee at McKinley? It didn't make any sense to me and I wasn't going to tell her any more.

I shrugged and she sat there, watching me, and I felt sorry for her because she really seemed to want to help but I wasn't cooperating. I never cooperated; it was against my principles.

"Our time's almost up," she said. "Is there anything you want to tell me?"

I told her I had something to ask her and she said that was all right, go ahead.

"How much longer do I have to do this?"

"Do what?" she asked.

"This, this talking to you stuff."

"Don't you like talking to me?" she asked, just like an adult, never answering your questions, always turning it around to trick you.

"You didn't answer my question," I said and she smiled as she imitated my sullen shrug.

"I don't know," she said and the bell rang.

Chapter 16

MISS Dickerson said I had an inferiority complex, but Grandmother said that was the most ridiculous thing she'd ever heard.

"She doesn't think anything's good enough for her," she said. "Not the other way round."

I think Grandmother was talking more about herself than me, but that was just the way it was in our family. Whenever anyone talked about anyone else, they were really talking about themselves. They'd look at me and see themselves; whatever I did was interpreted through their own feelings, without even considering that I might feel differently from them. When I wanted to be alone, Mother thought it was because I was hiding my loneliness and Daddy thought it was because I was independent and Grandmother thought it was because I was selfish and arrogant. They never even *asked* me, they just assumed, and they would have laughed their heads off if I'd told them I liked to be alone because it was the only time I could be myself.

It was hard, not knowing who or what I was, not knowing what was mine and what was just a genetic trait, handed down like some dusty heirloom. When I was good, they'd fight over me like dogs over a bone. "She's just like *me!*" they'd cry and I'd stand there feeling empty and stupid, like a mere bowl they molded in pottery class, to hold their brilliant genes. Sometimes, they'd even compete with me—I'd come home from school with my little drawing with the gold star and Mother would say, "That's nice, dear, did I ever tell you about the time I won the Michigan School Arts Prize? I was just about your age . . ." and I'd look at my little stick-girl, smiling under a stick-tree, and feel ashamed. I'd trudge upstairs, wondering why the teacher gave me a gold star when my drawing was so childish and stupid. She was just being nice, I'd think resentfully, wishing she'd given me the F I deserved.

Even Daddy had to compete. "It's the American Way!" he always said, but not with your *kid!* When I came home with the letter saying I'd been chosen for the Accelerated Program he patted my head and told me I took after him, he was so accelerated he'd skipped three grades.

When I was bad, they didn't know me. Nobody would claim my temper, my fits, my sullen lack of respect. They'd act as if I'd just flown in from another planet or try to push my bad behavior off on errant genes in the other's family— Daddy's crazy Cousin Leroy or Mother's Aunt Rachael, who ran away with an India Indian and was never heard from again.

It was bad of me to be so angry about it. "Oh, big deal," Cindy used to say when I'd complain about it. "Everybody's parents are like that. What have you got to complain about—you're the luckiest girl in North Bay!"

I guessed I was. My parents were usually pretty nice to

me, except when Grandmother was around and Mother turned into a podperson. It was as if Grandmother took over her soul and every rotten thing Grandmother did to Mother, she'd end up doing to me, not because she wanted to, but because she *had* to. She couldn't help herself and she didn't mean it and I could always tell she felt terrible afterwards. She'd cry and try to make it up to me, but she never said she was sorry. If she said she was sorry, she would have to admit she hurt me, and she couldn't do that.

It wasn't her fault. She just had Bad Luck, losing her father and getting stuck with Grandmother, and her bad luck was written all over her. "If only," she always said, "if only this and if only that." She ate and breathed "if only"; she exuded it, like perfume—she'd walk through the house, leaving behind a faint odor of regret, of loss, of promise unfulfilled and I hated that smell. Worse than skunk, worse than dog-do, worse than Frank Risdesky's garlicky house, worse than Hilary Kiley's grandmother's room, all powdery and decayed, Lysoled to cover the odor of death, to cover up the smell of life rotting away.

It sat over our house like a fog. It got in through our pores. At night, it drifted under the doorway and oozed into our dreams. Mother would have died if she'd known, for what she wanted most of all was for our lives to be better than hers. If she'd known she wasn't hiding it behind her smiles of attempted cheerfulness, her eager assurances that everything was fine, fine, fine, she would have been horrified. She would have locked herself into a leak-proof bubble and lowered herself into the Lake, to protect us from her own fumes. "I'm doing this for you," she'd say as she waved through the plastic peephole. "Don't worry about *me*. It's fine, really." We would sob and wonder who would cook our dinner, who would tend our wounds, who would get out the vaporizer when we had the croup, who would make our beds. "Oh, your father will find someone to replace me," she'd say, her voice echoing in the water. "You don't need me." And down she'd go, with only a few air bubbles to trace her descent.

It could have been worse. At least my parents weren't like Cindy's ex-dad or Mrs. Moore, at least they weren't like Mr. Ditwell, who would come home from work and toss Tom's friends out the back door like dried-up Christmas trees.

"We just want you to be happy," Mother said, the first time they threatened to send me away to boarding school. Part of it was true and part of it wasn't. There was a part of her that wanted to be rid of me, to get me out of her sight so she wouldn't have to feel bad all the time. And there was another part that really thought that sending me away to some East Coast rich girls' school would make me happy, but it wouldn't make *me* happy, it would make *her* happy. She wanted me to go someplace where I'd learn to be a lady and be with girls from quality families. Where I'd get a good education and come home quoting Homer. Where I'd get invited to someone's debut. Mother had this thing about "coming out." She thought that everything bad that happened to her was because she wasn't properly introduced to society and if only she'd had a debut, everything would be different.

Girls didn't come out in North Bay, which was just as well, because Daddy would never have stood for it. "What a lot of nonsense," he would have said. "We already *know* everyone worth knowing." Instead, they had Sweet Sixteen parties at one of the golf clubs, something I was dreading, even though it was three years and one month away. With any luck, I wouldn't have to have one, now that I was a pariah.

Chapter 17

TOM Ditwell wanted to walk home with me, but I couldn't risk it. What if I peed my pants in front of him? He'd tell the whole world and everybody would hate me more than they already did.

"I have a piano lesson," I lied and he said he didn't know I was taking piano.

"Oh, yes," I said, "I'm going to be a concert pianist."

I loved it when I lied like that, when the words came out so smoothly I almost believed them myself. The truth was, I had three lessons when I was six, but Mother took me out when I bit the teacher.

"Well, you won't forget about Rocky, will you?" he asked and I promised I wouldn't. He ran off to join Billy Jensen and Kenny Costello and I stood there, watching them, waiting to find out which way they were going so I could go another.

"C'mon, Goob," I shouted and she jumped up and ran over. We cut through the woods behind the Donaldsons' and I stood there for a while, looking at the swamp, wondering what would happen if I just walked right into it. Maybe if I went into the swamp, I'd get sucked into a slimy world and turned into a mutant, like the Creature from the Black Lagoon, and then I could spend the rest of my life living in the muck, waiting for school kids to scare. That was probably what would happen to me, something murky like that. I was as likely to turn out to be a Creature as first woman governor of Michigan.

I decided to go to the fort and watch for the Pervert alone, even though I was kind of scared to confront him by myself. The whole point of watching for him was to catch him red-handed, to save his victim and bring him to justice, and I wasn't sure I could do that alone. It would be his word against mine and who would believe *me?*

"She's lying," Mr. Diller told my parents after the trouble. "She's making it up."

My parents were sitting in the two naugahyde chairs in front of Mr. Diller's desk; I sat behind them on a low, plastic-seated bench. I stared at the photograph of President Kennedy on the wall behind Mr. Diller and wondered if they'd take me in the Peace Corps. Probably not; they'd take one look at my record and say, "This is the *Peace* Corps, we don't want troublemakers like you."

Daddy was furious. "I want him fired!" he shouted. "I want him out of the school district."

Mother was white, whiter than Mrs. Moore, whiter than Miss Nolan's nose. She sat there, ladylike, legs crossed at the ankles and with a corsage pinned to the lapel of her navy-blue suit, as if she were going to a Mother–Daughter tea rather than my execution.

Mr. Diller sat behind his desk, with his fat, round face, which normally looked so jolly and un-principal-like, scrunched in like a rotten grapefruit.

"I'm sorry, Mr. Pittsfield," he said, "but I'm afraid it's Maggie's word against his and I believe him. Maggie's . . . well, Maggie *exaggerates.*"

Maggie exaggerates. Maggie's got quite an imagination. In other words, Maggie's crazy.

Mother hung her head and Daddy fumed. "I can't believe she'd make something like this up," he shouted. "I think *he's* lying and I want him fired!"

Firing wasn't good enough for him, as far as I was concerned. I wanted him dead. I wanted him branded and flogged; I wanted him to be tied to the flagpole and kept there for a month, to be jeered at and pelted with rotten eggs. I wanted him to disappear and never be seen on the face of the earth again.

"The matter is closed," Mr. Diller said, getting up from his chair and dismissing my parents like naughty children. "Thank you for your time."

That was in April. From the Accelerated Program to Summer Detention, in two short months. Grandmother was delighted when she got up here and heard the news. "I guess *that* will take the wind out of your sails, Miss First-Woman-Governor-of-Michigan," she said gleefully, and I wished a tornado would hit and suck her right out the window and drop her on Alcatraz.

I cut through the Donaldsons' woods and then across St. Joseph Avenue, into Edison Woods. I sneaked through the Tuckers' yard and I could hear Cindy and her gang in the garage, shrieking and yelling and having a good time while they made toilet-paper flowers for her float. I wondered whether Ginger Moore was there and that hurt, thinking about her sitting cross-legged on the floor with a roll of yellow toilet paper, giggling and telling jokes, and totally lost to me.

It was a stupid float, anyway. She did the same thing every

year—there was a tepee and a big chair, decorated to look like a throne, where Cindy sat being an Indian princess while her squaws stood around her, dressed in brown sacks and looking as drab as possible, fanning her with cardboard palm leaves. It was disgusting.

It was really her grandfather's float, but he had a sporting-goods store and I didn't know what that had to do with Indians. There wasn't an Indian within a hundred miles of North Bay and nobody even knew what kind of Indians had been here, even though the local museum did some excavations to try to find out. Mr. Hilliard told me about it, before he got booted out of North Bay. All they knew was that they were either Potawatomis or Ottawas or Chippewas, but the French either murdered them all or sent them packing out West. I thought it was insulting to have a float full of white girls pretending to be Indians and if I were a Chippewa, I'd scalp 'em.

I made my way through the woods, towards the fort, wondering what the Pervert was like when he wasn't being a Pervert. He could be anything—a doctor or a salesman or a garbage man or an auto mechanic. He could be a she: a mother or a teacher or a beautician. "What makes a person a Pervert?" I asked Goob, and I wished Ginger didn't hate me so we could talk about it. My theory was this: something very bad happened to the Pervert when he was little and he'd blocked it out, but every once in a while, when the moon-rays hit him, he'd have this overwhelming need to act it out, even though he didn't know what he was doing. He didn't even know that he was doing to someone else what was done to him, because he'd forgotten. So he'd hate himself afterwards, but when he was in his Pervert state, there wasn't anything he could do about it—he had to find someone to hurt, to pass it along, kind of.

I almost felt sorry for him, but that didn't mean I didn't

want him tarred and feathered and hung upside down outside the County Jail by his thumbnails. It was his responsi-
bility, when he felt himself turning all ugly and anxious and
perverse, to lock himself in the bathroom until it was over
and if he couldn't control it, then he should just take it out
on himself. It wasn't fair to take it out on some kid who
couldn't protect herself, it wasn't fair, she should keep her
perversion to herself instead of spreading it around like lep-
rosy, creating potential Perverts out of her victims, it wasn't
fair and he should be punished, he should be made to see
what he was doing because the only person who could stop
him was himself.

I wondered if Mr. Howard was a Pervert. I couldn't be sure,
but I'd come as close to finding out as I wanted and at least
I'd escaped, even if it did mean getting kicked out of the
Accelerated Program. I didn't care; being in the Accelerated
Program was no big deal, it just meant I got to take Journal-
ism and Spanish instead of reading.

I hated him. I hated him. I'd close my eyes and see him,
sitting on the edge of his desk with his legs spread open and
his thing bulging in his pants for all the world to see. "Mr.
Howard puts a banana in his pants," Cindy had declared, but
I knew it was real. I hated it; I hated it and I hated him and I
wondered why nobody made him stop—why didn't he sit
behind his desk like a regular teacher, why didn't he stand up
at the blackboard with his back to us, why didn't he close his
stupid legs or at least cross them? Why did he have to sit
there, making us look at his stupid thing for a whole hour—
how could anyone concentrate on the five W's when he was
sitting there displaying himself?

I hated him with an uncontrollable passion: I wanted God
to strike him dead, I wanted him to fall through the floor and
descend straight to hell, I wanted him to sizzle and fry like a

pig at a luau, I wanted his eyes to fall out and his arms to drop off and his thing to shrivel up into a sickly worm and then what would he have to show off?

Cindy couldn't understand why I was getting so upset. She thought it was hilarious and drew little pictures of him, a bunch of sticks and a big banana, and passed them to Ginger and me and they'd both be giggling and Mr. Howard would get mad and that's how I got into the trouble at school. He'd been perched up on the edge of his desk, as usual, his tight trousers pulling as if they'd split and that damn thing of his bulging like crazy. Cindy leaned over and started singing, "Yes, we have no bananas," and I couldn't help it, I burst out laughing and Mr. Howard jumped off his desk and pointed his finger at me and said, "YOU!"

Cindy's eyes started popping out of her head and she kept whispering, "I'm sorry, I'm sorry," and Mr. Howard pounded on his desk and told me to stay after class. "I'm sorry," Cindy said again, but it was too late. I was too terrified to think about her—what would he *do* to me, out there in the Quonset hut, cut off from the rest of the school—he could do anything and no one could see!

The bell rang and the good kids filed out, staring at me, some with pity and some with glee. "Don't go!" I wanted to shout. "Don't leave me here with him!" but I didn't, I just hung my head in shame and tried to swallow the panic rising up inside me—what would he *do* to me? After everyone left, he closed the door and sat on the edge of his desk, with his legs spread as usual, holding his pointer in his hand and tapping it against his thigh. I sat at the back, petrified, trying to think of some way out. I had to do something, but I didn't know what. I needed time, I needed time to think, to figure it out, to talk my way out of it, but I couldn't think of any words and there was no time and I was like an animal, frozen in fear—if I ran for the door, he'd catch me. What would happen if I started screaming, if I fainted, no, not that, I wasn't blacking out ever again.

"Come here, Maggie," he said, but I refused to budge.

"Maggie!" he shouted and I crossed my arms over my chest and clenched my teeth and glared at him. He couldn't make me, I told myself over and over again. I longed to flee; everything inside me was going crazy and the voices were shouting and a voice louder than the others, louder even than Margaret's, a voice like a child's hopeless cry, screamed, *Don't let him touch you!*

He started coming towards me, with that sharp pointer, with his face all twisted and mean, and for an instant I truly thought he was a monster, some horrible fiend come to suck my blood, to take over my body and mind and make me into a zombie. He slapped the pointer on his thigh as he kept coming towards me and it was all I could see, that pointer, coming closer and closer and no, he wasn't going to touch me, no, I wouldn't let him, I didn't have to, nobody can make me, I wasn't going to learn a lesson, and I could feel that crazy feeling coming, sweeping over me like Niagara Falls, and I could feel my control crashing onto the rocks below. Margaret was coming and that meant trouble.

Mr. Howard whacked his pointer on the desk in front of me and growled, "I said, *come here!*"

Margaret went berserk. She started screeching, calling him names and telling him he couldn't *make* her do anything. "Leave me alone! Leave me alone!" she shouted as she backed behind her desk, getting ready to make a run for it. 'Don't you TOUCH me!'

Mr. Howard leaped over and grabbed for me and I tried to get out of his grasp, but I fell down and hit my arm against the sharp metal foot of a desk, cutting it and making it bleed all over.

"You *pushed* me!" I screamed hysterically. "You pushed me! You're trying to *kill* me!"

"Maggie," he said, nice now, now that the blood was gushing out of my arm like a river. Wasn't that always the way, they'd do something ghastly to you and they wouldn't stop no matter how much you protested, but once the blood started they got scared and tried to be all nice and comforting so you wouldn't tell. I wasn't falling for it. I wouldn't listen. I didn't want to hear his soft, oozing words, his *I'm sorrys*. Sure he was sorry, now that I was bleeding all over his classroom, but if it was all inside he wouldn't be one bit sorry.

"Maggie, please . . ." he said and I covered my ears and ran from the Quonset hut, into the main building, past Mrs. Sherman's room where I was supposed to be speaking Spanish, past Mr. Peacock in his janitor's closet, around the corner and towards the elementary section, down the steps and past Ruthie's room, into the little kids' bathroom. I locked myself in a stall and sat on a tiny toilet, sobbing and wondering what I would do.

My life was over. This was it, something too terrible for even Daddy to forgive me. I went back and forth in my head, thinking, It wasn't my fault, and then, It was! It was your fault! I didn't know, it was all too fast. Maybe I shouldn't have laughed at his thing. Maybe I did something to make him want to sit there with his legs open like a gate, showing off and making me sick, maybe there *was* something wrong with me; nobody else got hysterical, they all thought it was funny.

The only thing to do was escape. I could steal Rick Keller's boat and flee to Canada. I could take my savings bonds and cash them in, take a train to Detroit or Chicago and get lost in the crowd. I could go down to the railroad tracks and hide with the hoboes and have them teach me how to jump a train.

I felt sad, because if I quit school at twelve I'd never get into college and never get to be the first woman governor of Michigan, but it was probably too late anyway, no one would vote for me when they heard about my past. I'd be campaigning and suddenly Mr. Howard would appear, like a bad conscience, and he'd go on television and tell everyone I was a hysteric and a liar and a troublemaker and I would be disgraced and I'd have to run away. I'd become an alcoholic and live in a run-down boarding house in Lansing and every once in a while, someone would walk by the porch and see me rocking and say, "See that old drunk? She thought she was going to be the first woman governor of Michigan!" and they'd all laugh their heads off.

I was sorry. So, so sorry. "Sorry, hell!" Margaret said. "That man's a maniac!" "You brought it on yourself," Cotton Mather said. "You must have done something to provoke him. People don't attack nice girls without a *reason*." Katrina wanted to be a stowaway on the next freighter heading for Holland and Sarah wrung her hands and whined and Trixie didn't even show up. I just sat there, with all of them shouting like a mob, and I don't even remember who came and got me, who pulled me out of the bathroom and up the steps back into the old section, through the hall to Mr. Diller's office.

I don't remember talking to him. I don't remember anything more about that day, except walking home, alone, and feeling this strange pain in my tail-bone, as if I'd fallen off the trampoline, right onto the hard gym floor.

Mother knew. She was sitting at the breakfast-room table, pale and shaken, staring at me as I walked in. She was waiting for me to tell her, but I just said "Hi" and went to the refrigerator for something sweet to eat.

"Mr. Diller called," she said and I shrugged and said I figured he would.

"We'll discuss this at dinner," she said and I panicked—I

didn't want them talking about this in front of Donald and Ruthie, telling everybody how bad I was, humiliating me in front of the whole world.

I shrugged again and took my Coke and my cinnamon bun and ran to the Sisks' beach, with Goober flying at my heels, to hide and try to figure a way out.

Chapter 18

I was interrogated, with and without my parents, but I never had to confront Mr. Howard.

"He pushed me," I resolutely lied. I hated myself, but I couldn't tell the truth.

"I want the man fired," Daddy kept bellowing and Mother cried, not believing me for an instant, knowing I was lying. She didn't want to ruin the poor man's life, she said to Daddy one night in the sunroom, but what about *mine*?

"Why would Maggie lie?" Daddy wanted to know. "Why would she make up a thing like that?" but Mother wouldn't answer. I guess she thought Grandmother was right, I was nothing but a devil, evil through and through, so bad there didn't need to be a reason for it.

I had to sit outside Mr. Diller's office while he talked to my parents in private, and I wanted to die, sitting out there behind the glass windows, swinging my legs and awaiting my sentence. The bell would ring and all the good kids flocked past and stared at me, sitting there like some criminal on display, and I wanted to shrink into a piece of dust.

But the worst was when Mr. Howard was called in and he walked past me, ignoring me like a flea. He was dressed in new clothes—grey trousers that were baggy enough to cover him up—and even though I could never say anything, I felt vindicated. He *must* feel guilty, why else would he buy himself a new pair of pants?

I knew what he was going to say. He'd say I was "disruptive" and nobody would quarrel with that. He'd say I'd fallen and that he was nowhere near me. He was scared, even though he tried not to act it. I could tell—he was as scared as I was, but for different reasons. We were both lying, and it was just a matter of luck who they'd end up believing; a hysterical girl or a shaken teacher.

"They'll believe me," I told Ginger with certainty. "They *have* to. I have scars."

I trusted completely in Daddy's power to get Mr. Howard fired, to have him run out of town. I wanted him simply to evaporate, to not exist any more and I was sure Daddy would protect me from him, get him out of my life forever, not because of what he did or didn't do, but because of what he reminded me of.

Mr. Howard came out of the office, grim and pale, and I was called back in. I wished my parents didn't have to be there, listening as my verdict was revealed. In the event that Mr. Diller sided with Mr. Howard, I didn't want my parents to see me humiliated.

"You will no longer be in the Accelerated Program," Mr. Diller informed me. "You will remain with your regular class from now on."

"But what about *him?*" I cried. "What's going to happen to *him?*"

Mr. Diller shook his head and said it was none of my business.

"It *is* my business!" I insisted. "It *is!* Why do *I* have to be punished and he doesn't?"

Mr. Diller just stared at me and I said, "It's not fair!" I could feel my throat tightening up and I was terrified I'd cry, right there with all of them watching. Mother and Daddy were just sitting there, silent, and I felt horrible, ghastly, despicable for having dragged them into this; how could I have hurt them so, how could I have embarrassed them like this, how could I have been such a disappointment to them? I wanted to die for having shamed them, but it was too late now and I wasn't going to lie down and whimper like a kicked dog.

"Maggie," Mr. Diller said, "he didn't do anything to you. You're making it up."

"Don't SAY that!" I shouted, wanting to cover my ears, wanting to fly away and sail into the blue of the little flag in the holder on Mr. Diller's desk, wanting to abandon myself to Margaret or whoever wanted to take over, even Sarah— I'd fly away and let her stand there, sobbing like a lost waif; even that would be better than being there myself. But no one came out; I was on my own and there was nothing I could do but defend myself.

"I'm not! I'm not making it up!"

I pulled up my shirt sleeve and shoved my scarred arm in Mr. Diller's face. "Do you think I made *this* up?"

"No," Mr. Diller said, pushing my arm away, "no one doubts you were hurt, Maggie. But it's your word against Mr. Howard's and I'm afraid we have to believe him."

We? We?! I looked over at my parents but they were hanging their heads, as if they were the ones in trouble. Their refusal to look at me was worse than the humiliation of being called a liar, worse than having to look at Mr. Howard's thing, worse than having him come at me with that pointer ready to jab me. It was the pointer's fault, I wanted to explain, if he hadn't come at me with that pointer, I could have stood it, I could have taken my licks like a good soldier, I could have handled it; it was the pointer that made me crazy, but who would believe that? "What a bunch of nonsense!" they'd say and send me off to Lapeer.

Defeat washed over me like sludge from a barge and I gave in, knowing that no amount of protesting would do any good. It was over and I had lost and it was the end of the world for me.

"I think you should go home today," Mr. Diller was saying. "Your parents can drive you."

"No!" I shouted. "I'll *walk* home! I don't want anyone *driving* me!"

I stood there, shivering with rage, fighting to keep from crying. "I hate you!" I cried, looking around the room at all of them, wondering how they could all be so stupid—didn't they realize that something else was going on here? Didn't they know there was something I couldn't say? Did they really think I was so evil I'd just make up stories to get teachers fired; what did they think, that maybe I was mad because Mr. Howard gave me a B for Effort last marking period— who cared, I got an A in the class—what did they *think*? Didn't they care? They didn't even *ask*, they just decided I was rotten to the core and kicked me out before I could ruin the barrel. "I hate you!" I cried again and fled.

That was the first time I peed my pants. On the way home from Mckinley, early in the morning when everyone else was switching from arithmetic to geography, I took the short cut through the Donaldsons' woods and peed my pants. "There's no cure for bad," Grandmother always said and she was right;

I might as well go sink in the swamp, I thought, better to get it over with now than to go through life as an unwanted, lying little Pervert who ran around ruining people's careers. A weak little demon without power enough to control her own bladder.

Everything changed after that. How I made it through the rest of the school year, I don't know. I just went to school and pretended to be a person, doing everything I was told and ignoring the pain in my butt and trying not to open my mouth.

That was when I had to start seeing Miss Dickerson. "How can I help?" she said the first time I walked into her cubicle, and her voice was so soothing I almost cried, but I didn't. After all, she was an employee of the School Board, a hired head-shrinker, and it was her duty to get rid of children like me.

I had hoped that when regular school ended, everything would be fine again. The good thing about summer school was that Mr. Howard wasn't there, so I never had to see him lurking in the hall. Next year, he was going to another school and Mr. Diller called me into his office and told me that, as if he expected it to make me happy. "You'll never have to see him again," Mr. Diller said, but it wasn't enough.

"That poor man," Mother said to Daddy one night. "What a horrible thing to live down. I wish it had never happened."

Daddy grunted and rustled his paper. From my crack in the floor, I could see the top of his bald head, which was beginning to get sunburned, and Mother's feet resting on the footstool. Every once in a while, a puff of smoke would float across the room like a fat ghost.

"I keep thinking about his family," she said. "How horrible it must have been for them."

I hated it when she talked about that; it made me feel

horrible and guilty, like some kind of war criminal. I didn't want his family to suffer, I just wanted *him* thrown in jail and left there until his thing rotted off. When I thought about his family, I felt worse than usual. I'd envision his two little girls, dressed in tatters, standing on the corner in front of Peterson's, selling pencils in the middle of a blizzard. I'd see his wife, grown grey and weak, hovering over a campfire outside a shack near the river, cooking beans in a battered pot. And I'd see him, bent and dirty, driving around town in his rusty car, picking odds and ends from people's garbage.

It's all my fault, I'd think, believing my vision of woe; if only I hadn't got hysterical none of this would have happened. If only I hadn't taken his stupid thing so seriously, if only I'd been able to laugh, like Cindy and Ginger, if only I'd got out of my seat and let him hit me with that pointer, taking my punishment like a trouper instead of getting crazy and thinking he was going to *do* something with it. How stupid! How could I have thought such a thing? Of course he wouldn't *do* anything, it was broad daylight, in the middle of the school day, any minute the glee club would be coming in to sing—how could I have panicked like that?

I despised myself for my weakness, my hysteria, my wild accusations. I felt terrible about his family. But still, I wished him dead. Picking garbage was too good for him and I wouldn't want to see him hovering around on trash days, looking up at my window and shaking his fist and saying, "It's all your fault, you little vixen!"

"It's over, Marion," Daddy told Mother. "Why beat a dead horse? Forget it."

But it wasn't that easy. I couldn't forget it. Every time I walked to school, my insides started pulling at me, as if there was a huge claw inside me, grabbing my stomach and intestines and twisting them like wet rags. Sometimes the pain was so bad I had to lie down, right in the woods, on my back, perfectly straight, and then the claw would let go. On days when the pain was so bad I had to lie down, I'd end up being late and Mr. Blake would make me wear a little sign round my neck that said BEING TARDY IS FOOLHARDY. The first time I could have died of shame, but another good thing about being in summer school with the bad and stupid kids is that everybody's so used to being ridiculed and punished that nobody makes fun of anyone else—we just pat each other on the back and say, "Don't pay any attention to Blake the Flake."

Chapter 19

DADDY woke me up at six o'clock. "Maggie!" he said, slamming open my door, looking all happy and excited. "Rise and shine! The Parade's in five hours!"

I wanted to kill him. I covered my head with my pillow and asked him to please close the door, but he kept standing there, grinning, saying, "Get up! Get up! The early bird gets the worm!" and I wished he'd leave me alone, wished he let me go back to sleep and live in my dreams, rather than in the real world.

"Go away," I said as Mother passed by, and she clicked her tongue and said, "Well, if it isn't Miss Sweetness-and-Light." She told Daddy she had never seen such an unpleasant person in the morning and I wondered why, if that was so, she didn't just leave me alone.

She wanted us all to be happy; that was what she wanted most in the world and most of the time it was my fault we weren't. She wanted everyone to be cheerful and gay and when we weren't her world fell to pieces. I hated coming downstairs and having Mother chirping at me like some goldfinch, asking me whether I'd slept well; I hated watching Ruthie slurping those horrible colored cereals, the ones with the marshmallow bits floating around like chunks of curdled milk; I hated having to look at Grandmother's jammy red lips puckering up to insult me.

I'd fill a bowl with cereal and slouch down in my place and try to block them all out, to go back into the dreams that were floating around in my head like Ruthie's marshmallow bits, and I'd wish I were back in bed, back in my dream, even if it was a nightmare.

I had terrible nightmares, but I couldn't tell anyone about them because then they'd really think I was crazy. I kept them inside, like a family secret with no family, wishing the ugliness of them would fade away, but it never did. No wonder I wasn't very happy in the morning, but how could I explain that to Mother? I couldn't say, "Don't talk to me, I just had a nightmare about dead children with no butts." She'd faint, she'd turn all pale and gaspy and think I was crazy and wonder what she did wrong to have a daughter who dreamed such gruesome things and it would ruin her entire day. She'd worry that the dream meant I was going to turn into a mass murderess; she'd tell the Bridge Ladies about it and Grandmother would say, "Better get rid of her now, before she burns the house down with you in it."

"Good morning, dear," Mother said when I finally clumped into the breakfast room. "Sleep well?"

I grunted and looked over at Donald, who rolled his eyes and made a face. Ruthie was intently picking all the orange bits out of her bowl, piling them in a soggy mountain on her plastic place mat.

"Where's Daddy?" I asked and Mother said he'd left to go downtown and set up the booth.

"It's only six o'clock!" I moaned and she said, "You know your father," but no I didn't. I knew he liked to have things ready, and he thought being late was a crime worthy of beheading, but I didn't know him at all.

"He's really excited," Mother said. "He gets such a kick out of this."

It was true. Daddy loved giving candy to children. He loved making them laugh and seeing their faces light up when they got a Donniebar or a Ruthette or a Boobar. He loved being the Candy King of North Bay, loved standing in his booth, chatting with the parents. "Mr. Charm," Mother called him and he could really ooze it out when he wanted to.

"He wants you to be there by eight," Mother said and I said I couldn't get there that early.

"Why not? You're not marching."

"I have to do something," I told her.

"What?" she demanded, and I said, "*Something*."

She walked over and stood at the foot of the table, staring at me with that "What are you up to?" look that usually meant, "You're grounded."

"She's helping us," Donald said and I wanted to leap across the table and kiss him.

"Oh," Mother said suspiciously, but there was no point in accusing us both of lying. She knew we'd stick together like two soggy stamps and there was no getting us apart. She looked sad; I think her feelings were hurt because I didn't want to be with them in the booth.

"Don't worry," I told her, "I'll be there before the first marcher crosses the finish line."

I really wasn't up to anything. I just wanted to sneak down to Daddy's factory and catch the beginning of the Parade from his office. I couldn't go stand on Main Street with everybody else, not by myself. I knew what people would think. They'd think I wasn't good enough to have anybody to go to the Parade with. Or, worse yet, they'd feel sorry for me, poor Maggie, she got herself in trouble and now no one will speak to her. I didn't want anyone feeling sorry for me; I'd rather have them spit on me or throw turds at me than feel sorry for me, looking at me with those droopy eyes, pushing their pity off on me, weighing me down with cement bags full of it so I could jump in the river and sink that much faster.

Mother wanted to drive us, but I wanted to walk. I needed to be alone, to pull myself together after my dreams so I could pretend nothing was wrong when I went into Daddy's booth and handed out candy and had to be polite to the whole town. I worried that they wouldn't accept candy from me, that they'd come to the booth and wait for Daddy or Mother or Ruthie to give them a candy bar, that they'd turn up their noses at the Boobar I tried to thrust into their hands.

I walked along the beach as far as the lighthouse and then cut up to River Street, behind the coastguard complex, which was the cut-off point between the nice neighborhoods and the poor ones. To make sure everyone knew, there was a run-down trailer park right behind the coastguard property, filled with rusty old lopsided trailers.

From there, I followed the railroad tracks. A boy from Riverside fell and hit his head against a rail and bled to death, or so they said, but that didn't keep me from taking the short cut. There were supposed to be hoboes living someplace between the tracks and the river, but I never saw any. The closest thing I ever saw to a hobo was George, the old man who came round on trash day with his little red kid's wagon, looking through everyone's garbage for hidden treasures. He was a nice man. He always had stories about being in the war, about being in jungles filled with bizarre animals and golden temples and Japanese booby traps. "He's making it up," Grandmother would snarl, waving her hand in disgust, as if even talking to George would give me beriberi. "The closest he came to the war was *Thirty Seconds Over Tokyo.*"

George had a wife or a girlfriend or something; every once in a while she'd come along with him, in her red polka-dot dress and her silly blond wig, and they'd look through the trash, discussing the items as if they were shopping at Tiffany's. I liked them, even if they were hoboes.

On the other side of Elm Street was the section of town where the houses were grey and chalky from the cement dust. It didn't matter how hard the people worked on keeping their houses nice, they were constantly covered with a fine coating of grit. I only knew one person who lived there, a girl from McKinley named Polly Sanderson, who lived in one of the old Victorian houses that lined St. Joseph Avenue. Her house was directly across the street from the grimy little park that had once been the site of the French fort, but now all there was was a row of broken swings and a plaque.

Except for the cement, Polly's house was wonderful—it had three storeys and an attic as big as Miss Child's ballroom and all sorts of hidden staircases and secret rooms. I'd only been there once, because Polly was ashamed of her father, who had something wrong with him. He did weird things. He'd go out in the backyard and tie himself to the clothes-line pole and pretend to be a scarecrow. He was an old man—Polly was the baby of eleven children—and he seemed more like a grandfather than a father. When I was there, he was sitting in the corner of the living room, in a big red armchair, just minding his own business and quietly singing "Over There." "Maybe he's got shellshock," I suggested and Polly burst into tears and ran upstairs and never asked me over again.

I cut through the cement-plant property so I could walk

along the river to the Park. "Don't swim in the river," Mother always warned, reminding me about the boys who drowned in the whirlpools under the bridge to Canada. Every once in a while some suicide would jump off the bridge and their bodies wouldn't be found for months; they'd end up stuck on a dock near Algonac and one even floated all the way to Detroit. No one who had jumped had ever survived and, in a way, I found that reassuring. If things ever got too horrible, there was always a sure way out.

After the cement plant there was another area of little cementy houses, which was where Thomas Edison's house had been when he was in North Bay, blowing things up. After that, there was Inventor's Park, which was surrounded by lovely old houses—huge, gabled houses built by the captains of the ships that sailed the Great Lakes. Some of them had towers and widow's walks and I wished we could live in one of them; I'd love to have had the room at the top, in the tower, all glass with a porch all round it, where I could have gone out and watched the freighters or the baseball games in the Park or the summer dances on the observation deck next to the coastguard cutter.

Most of those houses were funeral parlors now. All along Main Street there was a string of them, and I wondered how they all stayed in business because it didn't seem there would be enough dead people to go round.

Prudy Taylor lived in one. She and her family lived upstairs and the funeral parlor was downstairs; once she had a pyjama party and we all dared each other to go down into the mortuary, at midnight, without flashlights. Prudy's house was beautiful but I didn't think I'd like living in a place with a bunch of corpses downstairs and I wasn't real keen on the idea of going down to visit them at midnight. But I'd never backed down on a dare in my life and I wasn't going to start then.

Prudy got out her Ouija board and we sat in a circle in her bedroom, asking it whether ghosts would come out when we went downstairs. Y-E-S it spelled and we shrieked and huddled into each other. "Whose ghost?" Prudy asked and I lifted my fingers from the marker as if they'd been scorched. "I think it should be a surprise," I said but everyone wanted to ask and I gave in. Prudy and I stared at each other across the board while the other girls read out the letters as the marker glided itself into them. Neither Prudy nor I looked at the board, not even once. "B!" the girls cried. "E! R! T! H! A!"

We were mystified. "Ask Bertha *who?*" Cindy demanded but the marker wouldn't budge, even when I gave it a little shove. None of us knew any dead Berthas and we couldn't even think of any famous ones, except Cindy said there was a movie with a Bertha in it, but she thought it might have been a cow.

We put on our slippers and silently made our way, single file, down the back steps to the mortuary. No one giggled. Prudy led the way, hunched over like some diabolical lab assistant in a horror movie, and we all did the same, making a little line of Igors, winding our way down to the lab-or-a-tory.

She led us to the basement door and opened it, switching on the light so we wouldn't fall. From the top of the stairs I could see black caskets and a big old marble table and I wondered if this was such a good idea; maybe we should go back upstairs and play "Twister."

Cindy was behind me, pushing. "Go *on*, scaredy-cat," she hissed, "you're holding up the line."

Prudy was at the bottom of the stairs, waiting, with a sinister grin on her face. Growing up around dead people, I guessed you got used to them, just like a beekeeper's kid wouldn't be afraid of bees and a farm kid doesn't mind the smell of horseshit.

It was cold down there, cold and stinky, like baby vomit. As soon as we were all downstairs, Prudy switched off the light and we were surrounded by darkness. Somebody grabbed my arm and I didn't care who it was—her hand was warm and human and that was good enough.

"Oooooooo," someone moaned and we all giggled.

Prudy led us to the big table and told us it was where her father prepared the corpses. Cindy wanted someone to get up on it and I shuddered with horror—what if they had planned this, what if they were going to "get" someone, what if they were going to shut someone up in a casket? What if it was going to be *me?*

"Let's go watch *Shock Theater,*" I suggested and Karen and Ginger thought that was a good idea, but whoever was holding me wouldn't let go.

"Berrrr-tha," Prudy called in a low voice, "Berrrr-tha. If you're here, knock twice."

Of course some idiot knocked twice and we all squealed.

"Berrrr-tha," Prudy moaned, "who arrrre you?"

There was no answer, but I felt a cold wind across my face, even though there were no windows in the room. I didn't care who was holding me, I was getting out of there and I didn't care who called me a coward.

"I'm going to go watch the movie," I said but just then Karen, who was standing near one of the caskets, started shivering and shaking like a fat woman on a vibrator-belt.

"Karen's having a fit!" Cindy cried. "The ghost got her!"

On shut up, you dink, I wanted to say, but nothing would come out; all I could do was stare at the blue cigarette-like smoke coming from behind Karen.

"All right, who's doing that?" Cindy demanded, in a voice so shaky I knew it hadn't been her.

"Karen's *possessed!*" Prudy shouted and we all made a dash

for the stairs, leaving poor Karen shaking and crying and saying, "I'm *not!* I'm *not* possessed!"

Prudy switched on the light and the smoke disappeared and Karen slumped down on the floor and sobbed. I thought it was a mean trick, but no one ever admitted to it and I never went back to Prudy's after that. I went home and threw away all my horror comic books and that was when I started sleeping with the Bible under my pillow. Prudy must have been playing a trick, I'd tell myself as I tried to fall asleep, but I was secretly afraid she hadn't, and that it had been a real evil spirit. Perhaps it had been looking for me and only hovered over Karen by mistake.

I still shuddered whenever I looked at Prudy's house and I wouldn't even walk on the sidewalk in front of it any more— I always crossed the street and walked through the Park, where I would be safe from Berthas.

Chapter 20

ON the other side of the Park, downtown started with a huge old building that used to be the high school when my mother was a girl, but was now the home of the local radio station, WNBM. Once, our Brownie troop went to the station to watch Milky the Clown do a radio show, but I thought it was boring. He didn't *do* anything—he just sat behind a glass window and talked into a microphone and didn't do any tricks or anything. Cindy got chosen to go talk to him and I was so jealous I nearly pulled her cap off.

"Envy is the lowest of human emotions," Mother always said but I thought it was the most common. You were never supposed to be envious of anyone else, but at the same time all the advertisements told you to go buy a new car so you could be the envy of your neighborhood, or to get a new washing machine so your neighbors would turn green with envy. It was stupid. You weren't supposed to *feel* it, but you were supposed to make other people feel it, and everybody went around trying to pretend they never were jealous of anyone else.

I was jealous all the time. I was jealous of people who did better than me at school and jealous of people who had lots of friends, especially now that I didn't have any left. I was jealous of girls who were pretty, because they'd grow up to be beautiful and I'd spend the rest of my life being "cute." But most of all, I was jealous of people who were happy and had hope and looked forward to life, people who were kind and good-hearted naturally, not mean-spirited and nasty like me.

I cut behind the radio station and looped back down to the river, passing the coastguard cutter, sitting idle at the dock, waiting for winter when some freighter would get stuck in the ice. Past Miss Nolan's white-pillared house over-looking the river and Park, past the medical center, to the YMCA.

On Friday nights, there were dances there for teenagers. Donald went to them and next year I could go, but I didn't think I wanted to. I was terrified no one would ask me to dance and I couldn't stand the idea of being a wallflower. But I loved to dance and I was pretty good at it. Ginger and I used to put on the soundtrack to *Bye Bye, Birdie* and make up wonderful, wild dances to "You've Got a Lot of Living to Do," shaking our hips and kicking and swirling around her base-ment like Mexican jumping beans. Once, Marvin Peabody was spying on us through the basement window and after-wards, every time he saw us he'd start shaking his hips and puckering up his mouth and I could have murdered him. After that I only danced in private, in the Black Hole with the curtain drawn, just in case someone climbed up on the sunroom roof and looked in.

There was a big lawn in front of the YMCA and then, behind another big lawn, was the County Jail. The carnival people were busy setting up their booths and their rides and I thought it was mean, having the festival right next to the jail, where all the prisoners had to look out their windows

133

and watch everyone having fun. They'd look out through the bars and see the flashing colored lights and hear the loud music and watch people looping around on the ferris wheel, and I thought if I were a prisoner it would make me even more mean, watching all those people flaunting their happiness in my face, and I'd hope the roller coaster flew off into the river.

I used to be afraid of walking past the jail because the prisoners always shouted things from their windows, but one day I started shouting back and now we were friends. "Hey, Sweet Thing!" they'd call. "What's doing?" and I thought it was kind of sad that the only people who thought I was sweet were convicts. I'd always shout, "What're ya in for?" and that made them laugh like crazy. North Bay was a pretty safe town; most of our crime was committed by wayward youths and drunks, although we had a murder once. A girl from Millersville was attacked and killed and her body was left to rot in the huge dunes of cement gravel. They never solved the case and everyone thought the murderer must have been a drifter, because who in North Bay would do a thing like that?

After the jail was the City County building and then after that the stores started, leading right up to La Salle river, where the Unemployment Office stood, all bleak and grey and depressing. I cut up La Salle Street and walked along the bridge, hoping I wouldn't see anyone I knew. I'd have to pass old Mr. Peterson Sr., who sat out in front of his department store like a living gargoyle, all humped and giggling and nutty as a fruitcake, but I didn't have to be polite to him because he wouldn't remember anyway. There was nothing anyone could do about him, sitting out there obstructing the sidewalk—it was his store and although he was kind of awful to look at, with his fat, pimply nose, he was harmless. If you'd sit on his lap, he'd promise you could go in his store and pick out anything you wanted, but Mr. Peterson Jr. always made you pay. Daddy thought it was hilarious. "That's some kind of salesmanship," he'd chuckle.

I walked west on La Salle, waving to Mr. Peterson Sr. from the other side of the street. I walked past all the little stores lining the quay—Mr. Polk's jewellery store, where I would sometimes buy charms for my bracelet; Fanny Farmer, where I would occasionally and guiltily sneak in and buy a Mint Dream, feeling like the lowest kind of Benedict Arnold for fraternizing with the competition; past the bowling alley, where Donald played on Saturdays in the winter and, finally, the pool hall, where all the yucky old men and delinquent teenagers hung out. Mother called it "sordid." "That sordid place," she'd say every time we drove past, as if it were an opium den or something.

It wasn't so bad—I'd been in, once, when Cindy dared me to find out if there really was a back room where they kept kidnapped girls to be shipped off to the White Slave Trade, but all there was inside was a couple of pool tables and a pop machine and a long glass counter where they sold cigarettes and candy.

There wasn't much on the south side of downtown, just the bookstore and the Ottawa Theater, which was full of bats. I went there to see horror movies, which were the only kind of movies I liked, except Bible ones. I couldn't stand most movies, especially the heart-warming family sort. They made me so upset I'd have to go hide in the bathroom and at *The Parent Trap* I even threw up my popcorn.

Next to the theater was Mr. Dotson's photography studio, where Cindy liked to stand and look in the window, staring at the brides and criticizing their gowns. "*I'm* going to wear my mother's wedding gown," she bragged, as if anyone cared. "She ordered it from *Paris!*"

I had no intention of getting married, unless it was to

Rocky Colavito. When I was really little I thought I'd grow up and marry Donald. "You can't marry Donald!" Mother had cried. "He's your *brother!* You'd have mongoloids for children!" but I didn't care. I just always wanted to be with Donald because nothing bad happened to me when we were together. I used to get hysterical when they'd try to split us up, when Donald would go off to school or to some friend's house and I'd be left alone at home; I'd cry and wail and cling to him like a suction cup. I didn't see why I couldn't marry him if I wanted. I wasn't going to have children, anyway, so what difference did it make?

Chapter 21

I turned up Maple Street, where Daddy's factory took up a whole block. It was a big brick building, a former fire station, and over the huge red wooden doors Daddy had a big sign with PITTSFIELD CANDY COMPANY printed out in candy-cane letters and "Sweet Is My Middle Name" printed beneath in curly script.

I went around the back and Uncle Herbie was out in the loading yard, stuffing candy boxes in one of the trucks. Daddy had given everybody the day off for the Parade, but Uncle Herbie never took a day off, not even Christmas. Working at the candy factory was the only thing he did and I felt sorry for him. He wasn't really my uncle, he was just an old guy who was kind of retarded and Daddy gave him a job stirring chocolate and he just never left after that. All the other workers made fun of him, playing tricks on him all the time, and I thought Daddy should make them stop, but he said, "They're adults, Boo, I can't make them do anything."

Uncle Herbie waved and I went inside and climbed the

steep steps to Daddy's office. I loved going there. Sometimes he took me to work with him and gave me a job, stamping coin wrappers with a PITTSFIELD CANDY COMPANY rubber stamp or alphabetizing file folders, and paid me seventy-five cents an hour and sometimes even gave me a bonus if I did everything perfectly. I felt so safe there, but only on weekends when Mrs. Greer, his secretary, wasn't there. She hated me. When Daddy brought me in and bragged about how smart I was, she'd glare at me and say, "Too smart for her own good, I'd say," and look as if she'd like to stretch her arm across the room, like a carnival rubber lady, and beat my head against the wall. Daddy just laughed, he thought Mrs. Greer was funny. "She doesn't mean any harm, Boo," he said and told me she was just "crusty." She might have fooled him, but she didn't fool me. I knew if she had the chance, she'd come after me with those pencils she kept in a mug on her desk, sharpened to long, black points, and even though they were Daddy's pencils and said SWEET IS MY MIDDLE NAME right on them, that wouldn't have stopped her from coming after me with a whole handful of them, poking and prodding and trying to torture me.

The Parade was starting two blocks up, at Optimists Park. I could hear the bands practicing and the horns honking and excited children squealing and I felt kind of sad and lonely. Life was happening, passing right outside the window, and I had to hide behind a curtain like a criminal. "Oh, pooh," Margaret said, "it's just a silly parade," but belittling it didn't help, I still felt cut off and an outcast and it didn't matter if what I was cut off from was dumb.

I could hear the cars coming and I pulled Daddy's big leather chair over to the window. The Mayor was in the first car, as usual, waving a flag and smiling. It was so weird, seeing Karen Harmon's dad as the Mayor. To me, he was just a regular dad who sat around on weekends watching the Tigers on TV and saying, "In a minute, in a minute," when Mrs. Harmon asked him to do something.

Mr. Harmon was followed by the North Bay Boosters with their "Young Tom Edison" float. They had a replica of the workshop where Edison experimented and the back of the float was a gigantic light-bulb-shaped piece of cardboard, covered in aluminum foil, with yellow crepe-paper streamers flying behind in the wind, like bolts of electricity.

Then came the McKinley Marching Band, with Rick Keller leading it. They were playing "My Country, 'Tis of Thee" to a marching beat and it sounded so goofy I had to laugh and get up and march around Daddy's desk, crashing imaginary cymbals and tossing my head like a majorette. I could do this, I thought, I could be a majorette, but then I remembered who I was and that even if I *were* a majorette, nobody would march in the same parade with me.

I stopped pretending and went back to the window, just in time to see Cindy and her squaws on their float, with Ginger standing there looking miserable while she fanned Cindy like a slave girl and Cindy smiling and waving as if she were Queen Elizabeth.

I decided to go downstairs and watch for a few more minutes before I cut through town the back way to get to Daddy's booth before the Mayor did. Uncle Herbie was still outside, still loading boxes, as if he didn't hear the music and the uproar and I felt so sorry for him I thought my heart would break.

"Uncle Herbie!" I called. "Don't you want to watch the Parade?"

"Oh, no," he said, so seriously I nearly laughed, "I have *work* to do!"

"Oh, come on," I said. "Just come see Donald when he

marches by," but Uncle Herbie wouldn't budge and I thought it was the saddest thing in the world, to have your whole life wrapped up in a bunch of candy boxes.

When I got out front, Miss Pocket's baton twirlers were in front of the factory, all sequined and crowned, with their little-girl big bellies round as beach balls. They were so darling, so happy and excited and thrilled to be part of the Parade, and I wanted to run into the street and gather them all in my arms and give them huge, sloppy kisses. I stood there and watched them tossing their batons up in the air and grabbing them and twirling around like sparkly tops and I loved them so much I couldn't bear it.

Casey Keller saw me and waved happily. "Maggie!" she cried. "Watch *me!*" and she sent her baton soaring into the sky, twirling around twice while it descended and then catching it behind her back, her face bright with pride and expectation, and I clapped and laughed and then all of a sudden something happened. It was as if an invisible hand grabbed me and knocked me against the wall of Daddy's building and reached inside and brutally turned me inside out and all the love and joy I felt watching the little girls turned into hatred. I suddenly hated their purity, their innocence, their happiness—I was disgusted by their joy and hope; I wanted to crush them, to blot them out, to squeeze their fat bellies until their guts oozed out like toothpaste from a tube.

I held my head and tried to shake the bad thoughts out, but all I could see were those batons flying around in the air, and I couldn't stand it, they were making me crazy and I wanted to crawl into the factory and slither into a vat of chocolate and die. Something horrible was happening to me and if I didn't get away I'd do something evil, something terrible. "You're turning into a Pervert," Margaret said, cackling like a witch, and I slapped my head with my hands, trying to knock her out, but she just kept giggling and saying, "Pervert, Pervert, who else but a Pervert would think such things about sweet little girls?"

I had to run away, to try to get away from Margaret's chiding voice. How could it be? How could it be that *I* was turning into a Pervert? I was only twelve.

"It's true," Cotton Mather said. "How else do you know so much about Perverts, if you're not one yourself?" He was right—how was it that I knew that inside-out feeling, how did I know what happened when they slid into that zombie world and couldn't help themselves?

It couldn't be true, it couldn't. How could it be? Something had to happen to make a person a Pervert and nothing had happened to me. It happened to someone *else*, but not to *me*, why would anyone want to hurt *me*?

I started running as fast as I could, down the back streets, past Weber's Dairy and the car wash, around Geriatric Village, past Trinity Church where Cindy went on Sundays to sing in the choir, "Like an angel," Mrs. Tucker said.

I must be a devil, I said to myself, how could I have such horrible thoughts? I had to run them out, run away from them. I'd better not baby-sit any more, I thought as I ran behind the old stores on Canal Street, and I wanted to cry— I was such a good baby-sitter and I loved the kids and they loved me, but how could I continue to allow myself to be around children when I had such vile thoughts? What if I did something? What if I got the urge to chop them up and stuff them down the disposal like that woman from Detroit did with her baby?

I had to get away. I had to hide, to keep myself away from everything good, just in case. I ran past the back of the bank, where I had my life savings, and wondered how far I could get on $250. I could get a job. I could be a child laborer somewhere, in some dark warehouse full of sewing machines, but even that was too good for me—I'd almost failed sewing and I could never get the bobbin in right and they'd find out and the foreman would come over and yank me off my stool and toss me out in the snow-covered street without a coat.

I could be a hobo and sneak a ride on a train heading for California and get a job at Disneyland. I could dress up as Minnie Mouse and no one would know where I was and at night I could sneak into the Enchanted Castle and sleep there and no one would know.

I cut across the Second Street Bridge to avoid the Parade. I could see the high-school band, marching across the Main Street Bridge to the tune of "Yankee Doodle Dandy," and I covered my ears. All the world was happy and bright and good and I was filled with this ugly, oozing hate and I didn't know what to *do*: I didn't want to hate anyone or anything, certainly not little bespangled girls, not the old veterans, hobbling along in their mothbally uniforms, so proud and pleased with themselves; certainly not the North Bay Boosters with their goofy lightbulb hats; not even Cindy in her stupid wigwam. Everything was good and pure and healthy and as it should be and there was no place to direct my hate except at me. *I* was bad; *I* was evil; *I* was darkness in a world full of light; *I* was a Pervert; *I* deserved it, I had it coming to me, it was all my fault.

I had to protect the world from me, from the possibility that the Pervent would come out and I couldn't stop her, that something would happen to trigger her off, like the trouble with Mr. Howard, and I'd be powerless to stop her.

That was it. That was the truth that grabbed me in the middle of the bridge and if it had been higher, I would have jumped off. But there was no point; it was too low, not even as tall as the high-dive at the Golf Club pool, and the worst thing that could happen would be I'd get a mouthful of scummy river water and catch some yucky virus, which was not the point. I didn't want to be sick, I wanted to be *gone*.

I ran to the water filtration plant and hid in a clump of bushes, holding my knees to my chest and rocking myself, just like Ruthie. I suddenly wondered if something bad had happened to Ruthie, if that was why she was so strange, why she stuffed birds and wouldn't go out of the house and rocked her bed against the wall like a bulldozer. What if what happened to her was something *I'd* done, what if I was already a Pervert, but didn't know it, what if I'd blocked it all out but had already gone all over North Bay, hurting little girls, doing horrible things to them, to my own sister! She was a pain in the butt, but I would never hurt her, I loved her, even if she was a weirdo.

Mother always said it was all my fault Ruthie was an odd-ball, and maybe she was right. "It's all your fault, it's all your fault," Margaret began chanting and I couldn't stand to think about it; it was too much and I started to cry, helplessly, not knowing what to do. "I don't want to be a Pervert," I sobbed, "I don't want to hurt anyone, I don't want this to be my Fate."

"Help me, help me, help me," I heard myself chanting as I rocked. Then suddenly I stopped. *Help me?* Who was that? Where did that come from? "Help me!" a tiny voice cried and I shook it off. *That wasn't me. That was no part of me*, I told myself. I don't need anybody's help for anything. I would never—N-E-V-E-R—ask for help, not ever. "Help me," the voice said again and Peggy's eyes appeared, two bright blue circles growing larger and larger. "What do *you* want?" I shouted at the eyes. "Get away from me!" but they hovered there in the bushes and I wondered if this was it, if I'd crossed over that invisible line between the real world and the Twilight Zone and at any second Rod Serling would appear and haul me off to the loony bin. I covered my eyes with my hands and prayed that Peggy would go away, that she'd just go back to whoever she belonged to and leave me alone. But when I peeked out through my fingers I saw not only her eyes but all of her. I was so surprised I dropped my hands and stared—Peggy wasn't a little girl, she was just a baby. Just a tiny, naked baby girl waving her chubby little arms madly in the air as if she were trying to push something away. Suddenly, I seemed to be watching a movie, and I saw her on a brown tweedy couch, just like the one in our sunroom that I hated so much. She was crying and kicking and her eyes just kept getting bigger and bigger as she watched something coming towards her. She kept making noises, as if she wanted something, and suddenly I saw what she saw: a bright blue knitting needle, coming at her, pointed right between her legs, and I screamed and jumped out of that bush like a rocket and ran for home. "I don't know any Peggys!" I shouted as I tore down the street. "That kid is not *me!* She's somebody else's kid, she is not part of *me!*"

"You're making it up, you're making it up, you're making it up," Cotton Mather shouted. "None of this happened." I fled home, thinking how upset my parents were going to be when I didn't show up at the booth, but I couldn't help it. Daddy's feelings would be hurt and Mother would be sad, and I was sorry about that, but I had to get away. It was best for everyone. There was something very, very wrong with me, something horrid. Nice girls didn't have visions of babies being jabbed with blue knitting needles; good girls didn't have a bunch of weirdo personalities locked up in a secret chest of drawers; innocent girls didn't pee their pants every time they walked home from school. Grandmother was right, I was born bad and I had to run away. I'd go home and get my bathing suit and my raft and paddle my way to Canada and escape to the tundra, where the world would be safe from me. If I made it across the Lake, fine; if I didn't, that was fine, too. Dead girl or outcast, what difference did it make? The important thing was to make sure the Pervert in me didn't get loose.

I tore through town, keeping my head down, flying through the Park and down to the railroad tracks, along the river, past the cement plant, racing home on instinct. I had to get home, I had to get away.

When I got there, all the doors were locked, even Donald's, and Goober was running around to all the windows, barking at me to come in, but I couldn't get in and I had to get in, I had to, I was turning inside-out and I had to get in the house before I went crazy. Oh, God! I thought as I saw Goober climbing up on the couch, wagging her tail and jumping. What if I hurt *Goober?* Maybe I'd better not go in! But then I realized that even if I did try to hurt her she'd just bite me and that would be OK. Dogs were better equipped to protect themselves than little girls.

I started pounding on one of the window screens, furiously, until it finally collapsed and I crawled in and fell on the couch and then the strangest thing happened. I got up on my hands and knees and started rocking, just like Ruthie, rocking and rocking and crying so hard Goober started howling, but I couldn't stop. I just kept right on rocking, as if I were trying to make the couch break through the wall and out into the backyard, rocking and rocking. "Don't think about it, don't think about it," I chanted as I rocked, but I couldn't help it and I got up, as if I were in a trance, and went to Mother's corner of the couch and took her knitting bag and grabbed all the needles and started jabbing them into the couch as hard as I could, pulling on the tweedy material and making it rip like long wounds, pulling the stuffing out and jabbing the needles in, crying and jabbing and shouting, "I HATE YOU!"

Chapter 22

THAT was the last thing I remembered. The next thing I knew, I was up in my bed and Dr. Keller was standing over me with a needle, getting ready to give me a shot.

"Oh, no you don't!" I screamed and I got so hysterical he put it away and said, "All right, all right, Maggie, calm down," and made me take some pills.

"You'll be just fine," he said but that was a laugh.

He went out of my room and closed the door, and I could hear him walking downstairs with Mother. I crawled out of bed and made my way into the Black Hole and got under the eaves so I could hear what they were saying. I looked through the crack and saw the couch stuffing lying all over the floor and Goober running around, sniffing at it, as if she were trying to find me in it.

Pretty soon they all came out: Dr. Keller and Mother and Daddy and Grandmother, and I could hear them whispering, as if somebody had died and they didn't want to disturb the ghost. I heard the door close and then Mother's high heels clicking across the floor. I watched her bend down and pick up some stuffing and I could see her back shaking and I felt bad, for making her cry.

"I'm sorry, Marion," Daddy was saying, "I guess maybe you were right. I guess we *will* have to send her away to school."

"*Reform* school, I hope!" Grandmother crowed. "You're certainly not going to let her loose at a *decent* school, are you?"

"Oh, Kay, go to hell," Daddy said and I almost cheered. Grandmother sputtered and then clomped out of the sunroom and Mother said, "Oh, Robert, it's so frightening. What do you think got *into* her?"

He said he didn't know. Maybe it was a delayed reaction to the thing with Mr. Howard. Maybe it had been tougher on me than they thought.

"Robert, people will think there's something *wrong* with her!" Mother cried.

"No, there's not!" he said but even I knew there was something wrong with me. Nobody would admit it because if there was something wrong with me it must be someone's fault and nobody wanted to think about *that*.

Daddy said everything would be OK; they'd take me out of McKinley immediately and start looking for a school for me. My heart leaped—well, at least I won't have to finish my stupid hero paper, I thought.

"It's not the end of the world," he said, telling Mother I could come home on holidays. He leaned over and started helping Mother pick up the stuffing and she started crying again. "May God forgive me!" she wept and Daddy took her in his arms and comforted her and said, "There, there, Marion, don't worry." I didn't know why she wanted God to forgive *her*—*I* was the one who attacked the couch and ripped it to pieces, you'd think she'd want God to forgive *me* for ruining her sofa.

"Oh, Robert, Robert, it's all my fault," she said and he said, "Don't be silly." I think she wanted to talk about it, but he wouldn't listen. "The past is past," he always said. "It's better to let sleeping dogs lie."

"Oh, Robert!" she cried out and he just stood there, not asking any questions, not wondering what she was talking about, just letting sleeping dogs lie. "Time heals all wounds," he said, sadly, patting Mother's back gently. "Time heals all wounds."

But no it didn't. All time did was create space. It moved the wound further and further away, but it was still there, as tender as yesterday, and all you needed was one reminder, one little pin poking into a distant scab, for the pain to come screeching back.

I felt terrible for making them all so unhappy. Maybe it *was* a good thing that they were sending me away; they could probably be happy without me around to stir things up. I was getting very tired. I crawled out of the eaves and went back to bed, pulling the covers over my head but leaving a crack so I could look out my window at the cherry tree. Daddy planted it on the day after I was born. "So you can grow together," he said and I wondered if there would be trees and a Lake where they were sending me.

I didn't want to get sent away, but there was nothing I could do about it and it was bound to happen sooner or later. It could be worse. They could be sending me to Lapeer; they could easily have me locked up with the loonies in some bleak windowless ward where they'd forget all about me. They'd fill me full of drugs or give me a lobotomy or something and then they'd let me out, when they'd taken all the parts of my brain that made me human, and send me home, where I'd be placid and dull, but safe. I'd be the loving daughter my parents always wanted and I'd marry some pharmacist or something, someone who needed a shattered woman, a woman who wouldn't talk back and make demands, reasonable or otherwise, and I'd have his children— children I couldn't handle, because having no spirit myself how could I meet theirs? They'd cut out my memory and, in a way, that would be good, because they'd cut out all my parts, but it would also be bad because I'd be a zombie. And that would be that. The end of my story: a lobotomized housewife, passively pushing my cart through Kroger's, pausing at the cereal section and trying to remember whether Junior preferred Cheerios or Lucky Charms.

Compared to Lapeer, boarding school didn't seem too bad. Maybe if I went away I wouldn't get into trouble so much. There would be nothing to remind me of my past and as long as nobody touched me, I'd have nothing to fear; as long as none of my teachers came after me with pointers, I'd be fine. Maybe I could start over, just like I wanted to, but without having to kill myself to do it. I could have friends again and do skits in the Talent Show and maybe even run for class president—Pittsfield for President! Why not? Why not?

I started feeling a little hopeful as I felt myself drift off to sleep. Maybe it wouldn't be so bad after all, I thought; I could go away and be myself and nobody would be chasing me around telling me how evil I was. Nobody would know my secret. I'd lock it away in my chest with all my parts and leave it here, under the eaves, and I'd go away and just be me, Maggie. No more Cotton Mather, no more Margaret, no more Sarah, no more Trixie, no more Katrina, no more staring frightened Peggy eyes, just me, *me*, Maggie. Maggie "Sweet Is My Middle Name" Pittsfield. I *would* be sweet, I'd be sweet and good and kind and loving and I'd even be polite.

I looked out at the cherry tree and thought about George Washington and how he never told a lie.

"Well, *maybe* I'll be polite," I said and pulled the covers over my head.

About the Author

Rebecca Stowe was born in Port Huron, Michigan, and currently lives in New York City. This is her first novel.